THE WRETCHED OUTCAST
VICTORIAN ROMANCE

Catharine Dobbs

Copyright © 2022 by Catharine Dobbs.

All rights reserved. No part of this publication may be reproduced, distributed or transmitted in any form or by any means, including photocopying, recording, or other electronic or mechanical methods, without the prior written permission of the publisher, except in the case of brief quotations embodied in critical reviews and certain other noncommercial uses permitted by copyright law.

Publisher's Note: This is a work of fiction. Names, characters, places and incidents are a product of the author's imagination. Locales and public names are sometimes used for atmospheric purposes. Any resemblance to actual people, living or dead, or to businesses, companies, events, institutions, or locales is completely coincidental.

Contents

Prologue 5
Part One 7
Chapter 1 The Consoling Garden 7
Chapter 2 Unexpected Arrivals 20
Chapter 3 The Dancehall 30
Chapter 4 Practise Makes Perfect 43
Part Two 54
Chapter 5 The Last Act 54
Chapter 6 A Parting Gift..68
Chapter 7 A Decision Made 79
Chapter 8 The Marvellous Marvolo........................88
Chapter 9 A Mixed Welcome...................................99
Chapter 10 Life on the Road 112
Chapter 11 Rowlands Park....................................122
Chapter 12 The London Show 135
Chapter 13 Hiding in Plain Sight 145
Part Three..153
Chapter 14 Home Again?.......................................153
Chapter 15 Performance of a Lifetime 160
Chapter 16 Difficult Decisions 170
Chapter 17 Parting is Such Sweet Sorrow 180
Chapter 18 The Battle for Rosedene 187
Chapter 19 A Secret Revealed 199

Chapter 20 A Happy Reunion 215
Chapter 21 A Crossroads 225

Prologue

Molly Walden was waiting. It had been a long night, awoken by the sounds of her mother's screams, the eagerly expected baby at last making its appearance. It should have been the happiest of days for Molly—a new brother or sister, a new life to love and cherish, the completion of her family—but Molly was under no illusions. The baby's arrival meant change, and even at the tender age of seven, she knew that such a change would leave her behind.

"We can only hope it will be a boy," she had heard her father saying, and he had made no secret of the fact he hoped for an heir, rather than a second Molly.

She had never felt wanted, not by her father, though her mother could be kind, if distant. Her father was a tyrant who made no secret of his dislike for the daughter he had never wanted. Most of the time he ignored her, but when his anger was raised, so were his fists, and Molly had found herself the object of that anger frequently. She had learned to stay out of the way, creating her own world of make-believe, rather than suffering the cruelties of the very real and unpleasant world around her. Hers should have been a life of comfort, her father the second son of a Baronet and with good fortune to his name. But life for Molly differed greatly from what it should have been, and she realised she was nothing but an outcast in a world which had never wanted her.

"Stay out of the way, child," the housekeeper, Mrs. Mallory, said, as she bustled past Molly with a stack of towels in her arms.

Molly stood meekly back, listening as further screams emanated from her mother's bedroom. Her father was there, along with the doctor, and Molly felt only an observer to an inevitability. If the child were a girl, then Molly would soon feel her father's wrath, and if it were a boy, she would find herself ever more pushed aside in favour of the son her father had always desired. Either way, the birth was not something she had looked forward to, dreading the inevitability which this sad day brought.

"Please, Mrs. Mallory, is the baby born yet?" she asked, and the housekeeper turned to her and laughed.

"Foolish child, do you not know what it takes for a baby to be born? You shall know soon enough," she said, and she entered the bedroom and closed the door behind her.

Molly glimpsed her mother lying on the bed, her father kneeling at her side, their hands clasped together. Her mother's face was pale, sweat dripping from her brow, and the doctor was shaking his head, even as her mother gave another cry of pain. Molly's eyes grew wide with fear–the screams, the pallor to her face, the anxious look on her father's face, it could surely mean only one thing, and Molly's eyes filled with tears, imagining the very worst…

Part One

Chapter 1
The Consoling Garden

Molly's mother died in childbirth. It was Mrs. Mallory who told her, taking her by the hand and leading her to the nursery where she sat her down and explained that the birth had been complicated and the doctor could not do anything except to save the baby.

"But you have a new brother now, Molly," the housekeeper told her.

Mrs. Mallory was not given over to sentimentality. She was a harsh woman, with a pinched face and narrow eyes, dressed always in black with a lace cap covering her grey hair which was tied up in a bun. She made no secret of the fact she disliked Molly, having always taken her master's line over the importance of a male heir. Now, she patted Molly on the arm and told her it was time to get dressed and go to her father.

"We are mourning?" Molly said, fighting back the tears in her eyes.

"Foolish child–your mother is dead. Do you not understand that? Yes, we are mourning. Now put on your black dress and go to your father. He wants to see you," Mrs. Mallory replied, and Molly nodded.

She could barely comprehend the awfulness of what had happened–her mother, dead, the one point of kindness in her life gone. She pictured her mother in the morning room, sitting in her favourite chair with the sun pouring through the window. She would look up at Molly and smile–absentmindedly, perhaps, but a genuine smile–and Molly would sit at her feet and her mother would run her hands through her hair and tell her she was a pretty little thing. To think of her gone, dead because of the child she had carried... Molly began to sob, and she collapsed to the floor, huddled in a ball, tears rolling down her cheeks.

"What is all this?" a voice above her demanded, and she looked up to find her father staring angrily down at her.

"I... I want Mother," Molly sobbed, and her father grabbed her by the arm and hauled her to her feet.

"Well, you cannot have her–she is gone, dead, and all thanks to you," he exclaimed, as Molly stared up at him with wide, fearful eyes.

"But I... why?" she asked, trembling in her father's vice-like grip.

"If you had been the boy, if you had been the son, no other child would have been needed," he cried, throwing her back to the floor, and turning away with tears in his eyes.

Molly scrambled to her feet, backing away from him, unable to understand the cruelty of his logic.

"But… please, Father," she exclaimed, but he turned back to her and shook his head, pointing his finger at her, a look of such anger on his face that she could barely hold his gaze.

"You were never wanted, Molly, and now you are even less so. I have the son I have always desired, and he will be your mother's legacy. Now get out of my sight," he said, his tone soft and menacing.

Molly backed away, fleeing from the nursery in a flood of tears. She hid herself in the laundry cupboard, remaining there for the rest of the morning, silently sobbing, her heart breaking at the tragic loss she had suffered. It was Mrs. Mallory who found her, hauling her out and scolding her for causing such worry.

"I have been looking for your everywhere, child. How dare you behave in such a way on a day like this?" she exclaimed.

The house was in uproar, the servants mourning the loss of their mistress, and a steady stream of callers coming to pay their respects and commiserate with Molly's father.

"It is worse for Molly, of course, she will feel it most terribly," Molly overheard the curate, Mr. Crockford saying as she stood outside her father's study later that afternoon.

"Molly barely paid heed to her mother—she is a strange and disobedient child," her father replied, and the curate tutted.

Molly hid herself once again, this time in a cupboard beneath the stairs, emerging only at the sound of her Aunt Sally's familiar voice when Mrs. Mallory opened the front door to her.

"Oh, Mrs. Mallory, I have just heard the dreadful news. Did Ignatius not think to send the kitchen boy to summon me? I had to hear it from the curate. How terrible, oh, how terrible," she exclaimed, and Molly quickly pushed open the cupboard door and appeared in the hallway.

Mrs. Mallory could not scold her in front of her aunt, though the narrowing of her eyes suggested she would save such punishment for later. Molly's aunt rushed forward and embraced her. She was her father's sister, and as different to him as chalk is to cheese. Molly had always loved her aunt and she in turn loved her, recognising the cruel manner in which Molly was treated and doing all she could to make up for it.

"Poor child, darling Molly, oh, how tragic, how terrible," her aunt exclaimed, enfolding Molly in her ample bosom, the scent of lavender, which her aunt always wore, filling the air with a comforting smell.

"She has been quite well looked after, Mrs. Fletcher," Mrs. Mallory said, and Molly's aunt turned to her and nodded.

"I am sure she has, Mrs. Mallory, but sometimes a child needs... familiar companionship in such circumstances," she said, glancing at Molly with a knowing look.

"I will–" Mrs. Mallory said, but the sound of footsteps coming along the hallway interrupted her.

"Oh, Ignatius, how very sorry I am, Lilibeth was such a darling," Molly's aunt said, still with her arms around Molly, who felt comforted by her aunt's reassuring presence.

"We must... make the best of things. Do not mollycoddle the child, Sally. She cannot be expected to mourn properly whilst surrounded by such sentimentality," Molly's father said, scowling at Molly, as her aunt straightened up and fixed her brother with a stern expression.

"Her mother died last night, Ignatius. I think there is a little room for sentimentality. And what of the baby?" she asked.

"He is in the nursery, the wet-nurse is here. You need not concern yourself too readily," he said, but Molly's aunt tutted.

"I shall concern myself, certainly, I shall. This is my niece and nephew," she exclaimed.

Molly's father and her aunt had never seen eye to eye. They disagreed on almost everything, and since their elder brother had died–his title passing to his son, Harold, Molly's cousin, an oddly eccentric man who kept himself entirely to himself–their disagreements had become far greater, still.

"You wish to see the child, I suppose?" Molly's father asked, and her aunt nodded.

"And I am sure Molly would like to see her brother, too," she said, glancing down at Molly, who nodded.

She knew that the arrival of a boy meant change, but she could feel no animosity towards him. He was the innocent party, unaware of that which he was born into, or the sadness which now hung over them all. He was a baby, innocent and unknowing. Molly was curious to see him, and her aunt now took her by the hand and led her up to the nursery, followed by her father and Mrs. Mallory. The wet-nurse was cradling the baby in her arms, but as they entered the room, she laid him in his basket, stepping back so that they could see him.

"A beautiful baby, Ignatius. He has Lilibeth's eyes," Molly's aunt said.

Molly looked down at her brother and smiled. Her aunt was right. The baby's eyes reminded her of her mother, and despite her sorrow, in that moment, she felt as though her mother was still there, watching over them both.

"Can I hold him?" she asked, glancing up at her aunt, who nodded, but her father shook his head and pulled her away.

"Enough of this nonsense. You cannot hold the child, no," he said, and Mrs. Mallory agreed.

"You are too young for such things, Molly, come away now," she said, and Molly glanced sadly at her aunt, a knowing look exchanged between them.

The baby woke up and cried, so that the wet-nurse hurried forward to see to him.

"Look what you have done, Molly," her father said, and he cuffed her around the ear.

"A little kindness, Ignatius, please," her aunt said, but her father only scowled.

"Kindness will not bring my wife back," he said, and turning on his heels, he marched out of the nursery and clattered down the stairs, even as the baby continued to cry.

"To the kitchen with you, Molly—it is time for your tea," Mrs. Mallory said, but her aunt shook her head.

"I will take Molly for tea with me, Mrs. Mallory. It would do her good to spend a little time away from the house. I will return her in good time for her bedtime," she said, and the housekeeper scowled.

She could not argue with Molly's aunt, and she left the nursery in silence, her footsteps echoing along the landing before disappearing down the servants' staircase.

"Can I really come with you, Aunt Sally?" Molly asked, and her aunt smiled.

"Of course you can, my dear–on a day such as this, you need to be enfolded in love, and there is little chance of that in this sorry place. Come along," she said, nodding to the wet-nurse who now had Molly's brother in her arms.

"I did not even ask the baby's name," Molly said, following her aunt downstairs.

In the sorrowful misery of that day, it seemed no one had thought to name the newborn whose cries now echoed through the house. Her aunt paused on the stairs and thought for a moment, furrowing her brow.

"I am sure your father will have a name in mind. This was supposed to be the proudest of days for him. But fate has a way of dealing us the sorriest of blows, even at times of the greatest elation," she said, shaking her head as they came into the hallway.

She took Molly by the hand, a reassuring figure against the sombre mood of the house, which, in its dark recesses and shadowy corners, seemed to reflect the mood which hung over it. Molly had never liked Wisgate Grange, the rambling pile which her father had inherited on the death of Molly's grandfather and to which they had moved from a pleasant house in the nearby village. It was the second house of the estate, set amid a great overgrown garden, surrounded by a high wall which ran down to the river. It was unloved and uncared for, filled with neglected treasures. They shut many of the rooms up, the furniture covered in dust sheets. Her father preferred his books to the company of others, and the strictness of his discipline cast a long shadow over both his family and the servants.

"I wish…" Molly began, the tears welling up in her eyes, and her aunt turned to her and put her arms around her.

"I know, my darling child—there is a great deal we wish for. But your mother loved you—do not forget that. She loved you in her own way, for she, too, had your father to contend with. I know him better than anyone, and I know he can be a heartless man. But you must cling to hope, Molly—the hope that things will be better, even if today you have every right to cry. Come now, we shall have some tea, and I shall do my best to raise your spirits," she said.

The day was sunny, belying the sadness which had come on Wisgate Grange and its inhabitants. The sun was warm on Molly's face, and the scent of the trailing roses above the door filled the air. Her aunt lived in a cottage on the far side of the estate, close to the main house, about a half mile down the high-hedged lane which ran towards the river, paralleling the gardens of Wisgate Grange. Trees overhung it, their canopies casting dappled shade along the path, where cow parsley and bluebells grew in carpets of purple and white on the banks. The shade brought with it a welcome coolness, and Molly could hear the sounds of the river gushing over the ford below. The path forked here, and

Molly's aunt's cottage—Rosedene—came into view, a low, whitewashed building, surrounded by a beautiful garden. This was her aunt's passion, and if the gardens of Wisgate Grange were neglected, here, they had brought nature into a seamless order—a harmony between creation and art.

"May we sit outside?" Molly asked, and her aunt smiled.

"Sit under the willow tree and I will bring the tea," she said.

Her aunt lived a simple life—she had no housemaid or cook or butler, and no housekeeper took care of her needs. She was an eccentric character, a leading authority on British butterflies, and she had travelled the world in search of them, her cottage filled with glass cabinets filled with curiosities from the furthest reaches of six continents. She cared nothing for the trappings of title or wealth, preferring instead to devote her time to her garden, and the study of the butterflies which inhabited it.

Molly liked to come to the cottage. It was a refuge for her, a place where she could forget the troubles at Wisgate Grange and share in her aunt's passions. She loved to watch the butterflies in the garden, to gaze at the curious plants, and to revel in the palette of colours which grew up all around. It was a haven and now Molly needed it more than ever. A tear rolled down her cheek and she sighed, imagining the sad fate which awaited her. What would life hold for her now she wondered?

"Will they send me away?" she asked when her aunt returned a few moments later with a tray of tea things.

There was a large Victoria sponge along with biscuits, and scones with jam and cream—Molly's favourite. Her aunt set the tray down before answering the question, pouring the tea through a silver strainer into two delicate China cups.

"Why do you think that?" she asked, and Molly sighed.

"Because I am not wanted. My father does not want me, Mrs. Mallory does not want me, and the new baby will grow up not wanting me. Only my mother wanted me, and only sometimes," she said, shaking her head sadly.

Her aunt handed her a cup and saucer, along with the largest of the scones.

"I will not allow your father to send you away, Molly. As long as I have breath in me, I will fight your side. Your father is… a cruel man. It is a terrible thing to say about one's own brother, but it is true, and your poor cousin Harold is so wrapped up in his own bizarre behaviours that it is a wonder he knows what day of the week it is," she replied.

Her cousin, the Baronet, was rarely seen, and the main house—Wisgate Manor—was, like its namesake, the grange, a sorry place, unloved and neglected. He was yet to marry, though his eccentricities would surely prevent it, and Molly had not seen him for many years, despite their being neighbours.

"Will he even know what has happened?" she asked, and her aunt shrugged her shoulders.

"I will call at the manor tomorrow, but he never receives me. The butler will pass on a message, but if we hear from him, it will be a miracle," she replied.

Their family was an odd one, and it was only her aunt who maintained any semblance of reasonable behaviour. If Molly had not had her, then she would have had no one, and it seemed her aunt had recognised this for herself, too. They were more like mother and daughter than aunt and niece, and Molly could feel nothing but loving gratitude for all her aunt had done for her.

"But you do not think they will send me away?" Molly asked, and her aunt shook her head.

"I do not think so, no. Your father would not wish for the expense. Besides, where would he send you? It is still far from usual for a young lady to be educated. He would not think you should receive the same opportunities as –though I only had a governess, whilst they sent away him and Lewis to Harrow. No, he will keep you here, though I fear for how he will treat you in the wake of this terrible sorrow. Certainly, I am sorry to say, he will mourn through anger, rather than pity. You must try to keep out of his way, Molly– come here whenever you wish, and if you do not come, I will know the Mallory woman has prevented it, and I will come myself to bring you," she said, cutting a large slice from the Victoria sponge.

Molly always found it amusing how her aunt showed no respect for Mrs. Mallory, always referring to her as "the Mallory woman," and showing only thinly veiled contempt for her whenever their paths should cross.

"I wish I could stay here always," Molly said, and her aunt patted her on the arm.

"And I wish you could, too, Molly. But your father would never allow it. I am afraid he means to punish you for what he believes your fault to be–not being the male heir he wished for. It is a tragic state of affairs, but it is as it is, and we must try our best to protect you," she replied, shaking her head.

Molly stayed a while longer with her aunt, sitting under the shade of the willow tree in the garden of Rosedene. She did not want to leave, fearing the welcome she would receive at home. But her aunt reminded her of the importance of bravery, and the two of them walked back hand in hand, finding the door to Wisgate Grange open and Molly's father standing in the hallway.

"They are taking her now," was all he said, as the heavy fall of footsteps came from above.

A moment later, six undertakers, dressed all in black, descended the stairs carrying a coffin. Molly clung to her aunt's hand, tears welling up at the sight of death now revisiting her, the horror of what had happened now overwhelming her.

"Mother," she gasped.

"Be quiet, child," her father hissed, his head bowed as the coffin passed by.

Molly watched as her mother made her last journey from the house. Words could not express how she felt, nor could they provide a comfort or consolation for what she had lost. Despite everything, Molly had loved her mother, and she knew it was because of her she had been so often protected from her father's wrath. She did not want her aunt to leave, clinging to her and sobbing, as she reassured Molly she would call again the following day.

"Do not spoil the child with sentimentality, Sally," Molly's father growled, and he placed his hand forcibly on Molly's shoulder and pulled her from her aunt's embrace.

"Be kind to her, Ignatius–there is no greater sadness for a child than to lose a parent. Did we not experience that when our own dear mother died so young?" she asked, and Molly's father scowled.

"It is a valuable lesson for her, Sally. Life is not always a bed of roses," he replied, and her aunt sighed.

"No, Ignatius, for roses have thorns, too," she said, bidding them goodbye, and glancing at Molly with a reassuring smile.

"Go to the nursery, Mrs. Mallory will see to your supper," Molly's father said, dismissing her with a wave of his hand.

"I miss Mother," she whispered, and her father grimaced, his expression turning angry.

"And if I could replace her with you, I would," he snarled, turning on his heels and returning to his study, just as the sound of the baby crying echoed through the house.

Molly made her way sadly to the nursery, curling up under the blankets and beginning to cry. It all seemed so hopeless, and she wondered if she would ever know the happiness which other children took for granted. The only glimmer of light in her life was the kindness of her aunt, and as she cried herself to sleep that night, Molly dreamed of the garden and of escaping into its embrace, of finding solace amongst the sweet-scented roses, hoping for something better to come.

Chapter 2
Unexpected Arrivals

The baby was named Tobias. It had been the name of a great uncle of Molly's father, and the day after her mother's funeral, they baptised her brother in the parish church, as Molly stood watching with her aunt.

"We yield thee hearty thanks, most merciful Father, that it hath pleased thee to regenerate this Infant with thy Holy Spirit, to receive him for thine own Child by adoption, and to incorporate him into thy holy Church," the minister concluded just as Tobias began to cry.

His father looked at him with disdain as he was being held by the wet-nurse. He had no love for children, but he would tolerate a boy, so long as he had an heir. He had made no secret of the fact he believed his nephew Harold to be incapable of a courtship, and that any child of his–any boy–would be the one to inherit the title of Baronet on Harold's death.

"Take him home, will you? I cannot listen to that racket a moment longer," Molly's father said, and the wet-nurse curtsied and hurried off with Tobias in her arms, as the curate came to greet them.

"Something blessed has come out of a tragedy," he said, glancing at Molly with a smile.

"There is still a great deal to be sorrowful for," Molly's aunt said, and the minister nodded.

"Life and death, we have seen them both these days gone by. And what about you, Molly—you must miss your mother terribly," he said, and Molly nodded.

"I do, sir," she replied, and her aunt put her arm around her and squeezed her.

"She will be well taken care of," she replied.

"Come now, Molly, do not waste time in idle chatter," her father said, calling Molly to his side.

Reluctantly, Molly said goodbye to her aunt and followed her father out of the church. It had been raining, grey clouds hanging inky and brooding above. Her mother's gravestone stood close to the lychgate, brand new, erected only the day before, and standing out against the aged, lichen-covered stones surrounding it.

Lilibeth Walden
Beloved.

Molly paused to look at the stone, remembering the solemn moment of the day before when she had watched the coffin lowered into the grave. She had wept bitterly, clinging to her aunt, the rain pouring down in sheets around them, the curate's words echoing over the graveyard.

"I am the resurrection and the life saith the Lord…" he had said as they sprinkled earth on the coffin.

She wanted so desperately to speak with her mother just one more time, to hold her and to be held, to tell her she loved her and to hear her repeat those words back. But the silence of the grave was all which confronted her, and now her father's voice called for her to hurry.

"Come along, Molly," he called out, and Molly followed him through the lychgate and out onto the street.

The church–Saint Nicholas–lay in the centre of the village, and several people stopped to offer their condolences to Molly's father, who played the part of a grieving widower well.

"And poor Miss Molly left without her mother," one woman said, patting Molly on the head.

"And what of her brother–deprived from ever knowing her," Molly's father said, and the woman nodded.

"Yes, quite so," she said, looking slightly embarrassed.

As they rounded the corner from the green onto the main street, a curious sound greeted them–clapping and applause coming from the far end of the village, and Molly peered curiously up ahead, watching as a caravan came into view. It was brightly decorated, like those of the gypsies who sometimes made camp on her father's land, but pulled by the most remarkable creature Molly had ever seen.

"Is that a... an elephant?" she exclaimed, remembering a picture book her aunt had once given her.

Her father turned to berate her, but he, too, now looked on in astonishment as the procession came into view. There were a dozen caravans each decorated in the same ornate colours. Horses drew the others, but there was no mistaking that they pulled the lead one by an elephant, which now stomped its foot and made a noise like a trumpet. Many of the village children had come out to witness this remarkable spectacle, and as the procession drew closer, Molly could see the words painted on enormous banners hanging from the sides of the caravans.

"Algernon Trott's Travelling Dancehall," she read, watching as several figures appeared walking at the side of the caravans.

The elephant stomped its foot again, and the crowd that had gathered cheered. There was an extremely tall man — the tallest man she had ever seen — ambling along next to perhaps the smallest man she had ever seen, who was dressed in a top hat and tails. Next came a woman, her hair almost touching the ground, and behind her a man whose face they painted red and white and who wore a bowler hat and polka dot covered suit. It was the most remarkable thing Molly had ever seen, and she stared at the spectacle in utter delight.

"Algernon Trott? What nonsense, what utter nonsense," her father growled, and he seized her by the hand and dragged her along the street.

"See the acts? Experience the excitement of the dancehall right here in Wisgate. See the amazing sword eater, the daring fire breather, the animals of the mysterious African interior. Roll up, roll up, for one night only. Singing, dancing, and delights to amaze you!" one performer called out, and the crowd which had now gathered clapped in delight.

"Can we go, Father?" Molly asked, watching as the caravans now disappeared off along the street and rounded the corner onto the green outside the church.

"We are in mourning, Molly—your mother is not yet cold in the ground, and you think it is right for us to indulge in such frivolity," her father exclaimed, and he cuffed Molly around the ear.

"I was only... it is just I have seen nothing like this before," she said, catching a last glimpse of the caravan turning the corner, the memory of the elephant etched in her mind.

"And you shall not, child, now hurry, I have heard enough of your nonsense for today," he said, and he pushed Molly roughly along, even as she thought how exciting it would be to see the travelling dancehall and share in the delights of the performance.

***

"Oh, Ignatius, what nonsense? She is a child of seven, it will be exciting for her. You do not need to come or have anything to do with it. I shall take her, I shall enjoy it, as will she," Molly's aunt exclaimed.

Molly had been listening to their argument for the past half an hour. She was sitting on the landing, watching through the bannisters. Her aunt had arrived to ask her father if she might take Molly to see the travelling dancehall. The performance was to take place that very evening in the church hall, and it seemed the entire village was planning to attend. Her aunt had bought tickets for the performance, one for herself and one for Molly, and now she was locked in a battle of wits with Molly's father, deploying both threat and coercion to get her own way.

"Frivolity—pointless frivolity. You did not see that awful procession—men making fools of themselves, freaks, degenerates—they should be locked away, not paraded on stage for the amusement of the masses," he exclaimed.

"You forget, Ignatius, I was once a performer on the stage," her aunt replied, and Sally's eyes grew wide with disbelief.

She knew nothing of such a past. Her aunt had always been eccentric, and she knew of her adventures across the continent, but she had known nothing of her as a performer on the stage.

"And the less said about that, the better. The embarrassed the family with your ridiculous antics. Running away to join a troupe of… of freaks," he said, banging his fist down on the hallway table.

"I am taking her, and that is that. The child needs some joy in her life, Ignatius. You have sapped any happiness from her by your cruelty, and I will not allow your actions to bring her any lower," Molly's aunt replied.

At these words, Molly got to her feet and ran down the stairs. She wanted desperately to attend the performance and to see the acts she had seen in the procession. She would beg her father to let her go and if he refused, she would run away. The thought had crossed her mind long before now—she would run away and never return. Her father looked up at her in surprise.

"Were you listening in on our conversation?" he demanded.

"How could she not have done when you have been shouting so loudly?" her aunt replied.

Molly's father scowled, his eyes fixed on Molly, who stood her ground, even as her hands were trembling.

"I… I want to go to the performance," she said, and her father's eyes grew wide with anger.

"Is that so?" he asked, and she nodded.

"I know we are mourning for Mother, but she loved the theatre, and we used to put on little plays in the morning room sometimes—when she was feeling up to it. She would be…" she began, but her father interrupted her.

"More frivolity—foolish women. Bah, go to your damned performance, Molly. But Sally, I am warning you, if this goes to her head, I shall…" he began, but now Molly's aunt interrupted him in return.

"It is a performance by a visiting dancehall, Ignatius, hardly the revolutions of '48. Do not worry, your daughter will not return to singing the Marseillaise," she said, glancing at Molly with a smile.

Molly's father waved his hand dismissively, and seizing her chance, her aunt beckoned Molly to follow her.

"Thank you," Molly whispered, taking her aunt's hand.

"You could hardly miss this—it is the talk of the village. Come now, before your father changes his mind," she said, and together, they hurried out of the house.

Despite the necessity of sorrow, Molly could not help but feel excited by the prospect of the dancehall show. Her aunt was right. It was the talk of the village, and all the servants from Wisgate Grange—apart from Mrs. Mallory—were planning to attend. The performance was not due to begin until later that evening and Molly and her aunt made their way to Rosedene, where they enjoyed a picnic supper on the lawn.

"What did you mean by your own performances on stage?" Molly asked, curious to know more about what her aunt had meant.

Her aunt looked up from her supper and blushed.

"Your father's shame—though not the rest of the family. They thought it rather… quaint, I suppose. When I was younger, Molly, I loved to sing. I was quite good, even if I do say so myself. Your grandmother would play the pianoforte and I would sing. I used to imagine myself on stage and I was often called on to entertain visiting guests at the manor house," she replied.

Molly smiled at the thought of her aunt performing. She had never heard her sing, though she would hum snatches of long forgotten tunes, her face coming alive with a smile as though evoking long forgotten memories.

"But did you ever perform on stage?" Molly asked, and her aunt nodded.

"Oh yes, that was what your father referred to—a visiting dancehall, much like this one, came to Wisgate. Being the sort of child who liked to push themselves forward, I declared I was going to sing, and sing, I did. Much to your father's embarrassment and the delight of everyone else," she replied, smiling at Molly, who gazed at her with wide-eyed admiration.

"But what about now?" Molly asked, and her aunt looked at her in surprise.

"What do you mean?" she asked.

"Would you still sing?" Molly replied, and her aunt blushed.

"I would still like to, though I am not sure who would wish to listen," she said.

"I would," Molly said.

The thought of her aunt performing on the stage fascinated her, and she would dearly have loved to listen to her sing. Molly, too, liked to sing, though she knew only snatches of ditties she had overheard the servants singing, along with hymns she had sung in church. She had always wondered where such pleasure came from, and now she knew the source. She wanted desperately to find out more.

"Well, perhaps I could try," her aunt replied, and she rose to her feet, clearing her throat and making a strange noise which sounded like "mimimimimimi."

"What will you sing?" Molly asked, gazing up at her aunt in expectant delight.

"A song about love," she replied, clearing her throat and beginning to sing.

"I have loved flowers that fade,
Within whose magic tents
Rich hues have marriage made
With sweet immemorial scents:
A joy of love at sight,—
A honeymoon delight,

That ages in an hour:—
My song be like a flower."

The words were lyrical, the tune soft and sweet, and the music filled the garden with such a beautiful sound that Molly found herself entranced. She smiled up at her aunt, shaking her head in amazement as she took a slight bow, an embarrassed look coming over her face.

"I am a little rusty," she said, but Molly clapped her hands together in delight, leaping to her feet and throwing her arms around her aunt, who blushed.

"You were wonderful. I had never imagined you could sing like that. Why do you not perform any longer?" she asked.

It seemed such a terrible waste for a talent such as this to lie hidden under a bushel. Her aunt was as good as any performer Molly had ever heard–though granted, she had heard few performers in her brief life, but of those she knew, her aunt was surely the best.

"I suppose I was… embarrassed to do so. Your father put a dent in my confidence – he told me I could not sing and that I had disgraced the family by doing so. It was not the path I was supposed to take and I… well, I felt as though I could no longer perform," she said, shaking her head sadly.

"Well, I know you can," Molly replied, and her aunt smiled.

"It means a lot to hear you say that. But come now, we shall be late for the performance – you are in for a real treat, Molly. I have been looking forward to this ever since I heard the dancehall troupe had arrived in Wisgate," she said, offering Molly her hand.

Chapter 3
The Dancehall

Molly had never seen the church hall so busy. Every seat, every nook and cranny taken. They drew the red velvet curtains across the stage, their gold trim freshly repaired for the performance, and there was an air of eager anticipation, as the hushed voices of the audience waited expectantly. Molly and her aunt found two seats close to the front, next to the curate and his wife, who greeted them warmly.

"I am only here, you understand, to ensure there is nothing pertaining to vice or debauchery taking place in the church hall," the minister said, and Molly's aunt smiled.

"Oh, really, Mr. Crockford, allow yourself to enjoy it—we were not made for sorrow, but for joy," she said, and the curate smiled.

"You are right, Mrs. Fletcher—it would be a dour world if pleasure were not a part of it – in moderation, of course," he replied.

"Oh, nonsense, Mrs. Fletcher. He has been looking forward to it ever since the elephant paraded past the vicarage the other day. Do not believe a word he says," the curate's wife said, smiling at Molly's aunt, who laughed.

"I think the entire village has been looking forward to it. I know I have," she replied.

At that moment, there was a twitching behind the curtain, and a slight parting in the middle, as a face peered out and grinned. Molly watched in fascination as the man—or woman, for it was hard to tell—contorted their features before sticking out their tongue, much to the mirth of the audience. Suddenly the curtains were flung wide and the man—for it was now unmistakably a man—cartwheeled forward and sprang to his feet, leaping high into the air, as half a dozen other acrobats appeared on the stage, cartwheeling, somersaulting, and contorting themselves as a musical ensemble struck up a lively tune. A moment later, the performers had arranged themselves into a human pyramid, and applause went up from the audience, Molly and her aunt joining in enthusiastically.

"Oh my, how brave, how marvellous, did you see that?" the curate exclaimed, turning to Molly and her aunt with an ecstatic look on his face.

But the acrobatics were only at the beginning of the performance. Next on stage there appeared the extremely tall man Molly had seen walking by the side of the caravans, accompanied by the very short man who was wearing a pirate's costume with a patch over his eye and a stuffed parrot on his shoulder. They performed an act involving much leaping about, ending with the short man on the taller man's shoulders, and a song called "the lament of Captain Black" which elicited much mirth from the audience owing to its somewhat bawdy lyrics.

"Cover your ears, Mr. Crockford," Molly's aunt said, but the curate was in fits of laughter, and all thought of vice had quite disappeared from his mind.

It was the most marvellous spectacle which Molly had ever seen, and she clapped along in delight as unique acts appeared on stage–some singing, some dancing, some performing. There were animals, too–slithering snakes emerging from a basket at the playing of a pipe, a remarkable lizard which turned different colours as it stalked across the stage. But Molly's favourite act was the fire eater, a man named Mr. Marvolo.

"My lords, ladies, and gentleman, we present the marvellous, Mr. Marvolo–fire breather extraordinaire, who, for your delectation, is to breathe forth flames before your very eyes. Marvel at him," the master of ceremonies declared, and Mr. Marvolo appeared on the stage.

They dressed him in a long black cape with a red silk inlay and wore a top hat on his head. They covered his eyes with a black mask with slits cut into the front. He had a waistcoat on with a golden pocket watch and chain at the breast and wore a bow tie at his neck so that he appeared dressed as if for the theatre. With a flourish, he removed his cloak, dropping it to the floor, and holding up his hands for silence.

"My friends," he began, in a silky soft Italian voice, "what you are about to witness is more dangerous than any snake charm, more daring than any acrobatics, more remarkable than any creature you will see-tall or short. Yes, what you are about to see defies nature itself. You will ask, how does this man do what he is about to do? How does he not find himself consumed by the flames he breathes? That is the mystery of Mr. Marvolo. Watch now, and be amazed," he said, bowing with a flourish, before taking a deep breath, concentrating, his head bowed.

Molly took hold of her aunt's hand, fearful of what was about to happen.

"How splendid," the curate exclaimed, as Mr. Marvolo turned and beckoned his assistant onto the stage.

A woman dressed all in black, her head covered with a veil, appeared, carrying with her a burning torch. The church hall was in darkness, and the flames cast flickering shadows on the walls as Mr. Marvolo took the torch in his hands.

"He cannot," Molly whispered, unable to take her eyes off the man, who now raised the flaming torch over his head.

He opened his mouth, plunging the torch down with a thrust of his hand, withdrawing it immediately and turning to the audience. Now, he opened his mouth so that the flames shot out like a dragon breathing fire. The audience were on their feet, cheering, as Mr. Marvolo took a bow.

"Again?" he asked, and the audience cried out, clamouring for a repeat of the performance.

The black-clad assistant again passed the flaming torch to him and Mr. Marvolo plunged it into his mouth, breathing out the flames high into the air. Molly's eyes grew wide with astonishment—how did he not burn himself, or set himself alight? But the performer only took a bow, delighting in the audience's adulation who were applauding rapturously.

"My friends, pray. Silence for a moment. I shall perform one final feat, something so dangerous that it has never been attempted," he said, smiling as though the truth was perhaps somewhat different.

"How can it be any more dangerous?" Molly whispered.

"He is going to be tied up, watch," her aunt replied, and Mr. Marvolo now held up his hands.

"I, the great Mr. Marvolo, will be bound hands and feet. My assistant will then offer me the flames to eat, and I shall demonstrate to you the fullness of my art by holding the flames in my mouth before using them to cut the cords which bind me. Can I do it?" he asked, and the audience shouted out in response.

"It is madness," one man cried.

"But it will set you alight," another said.

"Ye of little faith, but watch now and see," Mr. Marvolo replied.

His assistant made a great show of tying the knots, demonstrating how tightly Mr. Marvolo was bound. He could not move, and now he stood at the centre of the stage, rigid and at attention. The flames were carried ceremoniously forward, and Mr. Marvolo opened his mouth. Molly could hardly watch, and she closed her eyes, burying her head in her aunt's shoulder even as she was desperate to see what happened next.

"Watch Molly—you may never see this again," her aunt implored her.

As Molly turned, Mr. Marvolo took the flaming torch in his mouth, his assistant holding it in place before stepping back. The audience held its breath, and Mr. Marvolo raised his hands in front of him, showing them the knots, before suddenly opening his mouth and letting out a plume of flames. In a flash, the knots were dissolved, and he threw open his arms as the audience cheered.

"Oh, bravo, bravo, how utterly wonderful!" Mr. Crockford exclaimed, as now Mr. Marvolo bowed.

But as he did so, a further plume of flames emerged from his mouth and the cords which bound his feet were gone. He leaped forward, cartwheeled to the front of the stage, and took a bow. Molly was on her feet, cheering with the rest of the crowd. She was amazed by what she had seen and could not imagine how such a feat could be performed.

"Can you believe it?" she asked her aunt, shaking her head in amazement.

"That is the wonder of such acts—we see them with our very eyes, but we cannot for the life of us understand how they accomplish their remarkable feats," she replied.

Molly had never seen anything like this, and it entirely caught her up in the dancehall's magic. It was no wonder her aunt had been so taken with it when she, too, was a child, and Molly imagined herself on the stage, performing alongside the likes of Mr. Marvolo and the acrobats.

"I want to perform," she said, and her aunt smiled at her.

"I am glad to hear you say that, Molly, and I am glad tonight has brought you happiness," she replied.

As the performance ended, Molly felt as though she could happily have stayed in that audience forever. She wanted to see the whole show again, and it was a wrench to tear herself away after the spectacular finale in which all the performers had appeared on stage to sing a final song, culminating in another human pyramid and a breath of flames from Mr. Marvolo.

"Absolutely splendid, I shall never forget it," Mr. Crockford said as they emerged from the church hall.

It was growing dark now, but the village green was busy with revellers, all of them talking excitedly about what they had just witnessed.

"When will they come again?" one woman asked, her face a picture of delight.

"Not for several years now, Mrs. Swanson, they travel the length of the country, and we must wait our turn in patience," Molly's aunt replied.

"Is that true?" Molly asked, as they walked home a few minutes later. "Do they really only come here every few years?"

"It is sometimes even longer, Molly. They have many places to visit, and it would be unfair to deprive other people of their remarkable talents," she replied.

Molly felt disappointed. She wanted to see the entire show again, to marvel at Mr. Marvolo and his fire breathing. She had seen nothing like it, and the thought of having to wait so long to see it again made her feel dejected.

"But I would dearly like to see them again," she said, and her aunt smiled.

"You will do—but you will just have to wait. Now, come back to Rosedene and we shall have some cocoa. There is something I want to show you," her aunt replied.

It was dark by the time they reached the cottage, and Molly's aunt struck a match and began lighting candles all around the parlour. The room was comfortably furnished, filled with trinkets and trophies from Molly's aunt's travels around the world. The butterfly collection in the glass cases looked eerie in the candlelight, the outlines of the wings appearing as though they might take flight at any moment.

"Which was the hardest butterfly to catch?" Molly asked, and her aunt turned to her and smiled.

"No butterfly wishes to be caught, but "teinopalpus imperialis"–the emperor of India. The beautiful blue specimen in that case over there," her aunt said, pointing to a small case on the far wall.

Molly peered through the glass, gazing at the small blue butterfly pinioned to the felt. It was beautiful, and she imagined it fluttering in the air, her aunt swiping at it with her net.

"Remarkable," she said, as her aunt brought the cups of cocoa to the table.

"Found in the eastern Himalaya. We trekked for two months into the foothills–it was a most remarkable journey," she replied, smiling at Molly, who took the cup and breathed in the sweet aroma.

"There is so much I want to ask you," she said, and her aunt shook her head and laughed.

"I have led an interesting life–and you, too, can lead such a life, Molly," she replied.

Molly took a sip of cocoa and pondered these words. She did not particularly care for her own life, and even at the tender age of seven, she realised just how hard life could be. She thought of her father and what he would say if she ever announced an intention to make journeys like her aunt had done or perform on the stage like Mr. Marvolo and the others.

"I do not think my father would ever allow it," she said, but her aunt furrowed her brow and frowned.

"Never allow your father to destroy your dreams, Molly. He is a cruel man, and I say that as his sister. He will crush you if you allow him to do so. Never stop dreaming, Molly. The time is not yet right for women who dream—I was lucky, my husband, your uncle, believed a woman should dream. We had such adventures together, and though he died very young, I would not change a single day we had together. You, too, must hold on to your dreams, Molly. Whatever they might be," she said, and Molly nodded.

She did not fully understand what her aunt meant, but she had the feeling that what she was saying was something meaningful and profound. Molly had many dreams—she lived her life in a dream of sorts, one in which she could escape the cruel hand and words of her father. She dreamed of running away, of adventures in far-off lands, like those she read about in the story books her aunt had bought her, and that night, she knew she would dream of the dancehall and the marvellous things she had seen there.

"I will try," Molly said, taking another sip of cocoa.

Her aunt set down her cup and crossed over to a cupboard by the stairs which led to the bedrooms above. She opened it and peered inside. It was filled with boxes, and she took one of them down and blew the dust off it, sneezing as she did so.

"There, now, you can see how long it is since I last looked in here," she said, smiling at Molly as she brought the box over to the table.

"What is it?" Molly asked.

The box was nothing remarkable—leather bound and with her aunt's maiden initials on the top.

"We all had one of these boxes, your father, your uncle, and I. I do not know what they put in theirs, but in mine…" she said, lifting the lid so that Molly could peer inside.

Her eyes grew wide at the sight of what was now before her, and a smile broke out over her face.

"But I thought you only sang?" she said, and her aunt blushed.

"I performed–juggling balls, costumes, singing, dancing– my total act is here, and I want you to have it. There is makeup in there, too. You will look quite the part. You can take them home with you and practise," she said, taking out the juggling balls.

She threw them up in the air, juggling them in three as she did so. Molly watched in amazement.

"I did not know you could juggle," she exclaimed, realising that the evening had been one of remarkable revelation.

"It would not do for us to know everything about everybody. Is it not pleasant to discover things about someone?" she asked, and Molly nodded, eager to try the juggling balls for herself.

"May I have a go?" she asked, and her aunt nodded.

"First try with two," she said, throwing Molly first one, then another of the juggling balls, and watching as she threw them up in the air and passed them between her hands.

"I think I can do it," Molly said, and her aunt nodded.

"Now, try a third," she said, and she tossed the remaining ball into the fray.

But with this ball came disaster and Molly could not catch the first two before the third joined them. The balls went flying this way and that, one of them falling to the ground, another landing on the table, and the third going straight towards the glass cabinet containing teinopalpus imperialis. Her aunt's hand shot out, catching the ball just before it hit the glass. Molly breathed a sigh of relief, and her aunt grinned at her.

"Perhaps just two to begin with," Molly said, and her aunt nodded.

"You will soon get the hang of it. Then you can try juggling other things, or dancing as you juggle, or singing, or whatever talent you can think of. That is the art of performance, Molly – knowing just how to delight your audience with something new and exciting. Mr. Marvolo has perfected an act which is quite remarkable, but he must always practise it and think of new ways to display his talent. You will be the same," she replied.

Molly could not wait to get started. She thought of performing on stage, of emulating the performers she had seen that evening, and even of creating her own act to wow an audience. The evening had opened up a wealth of possibility and taken her mind off her troubles in the here and now.

"Can I really have these things? What if you wanted to practise with them yourself?" she said, and her aunt laughed.

"Such days are over for me. I will be content to watch you, instead. Why not practise a performance and we shall have our own dancehall here at Rosedene. I can sing, and perhaps even dance, and you can show me what you have taught yourself. We will dust off the piano and make a stage in the corner. Would you like that?" she asked, and Molly nodded.

"I would like it very much, Aunt Sally," she said, and her aunt smiled.

"Then it shall be our secret, Molly, and we will set aside the cares of this world for a few hours at least. But come now, we must get you home. I will be in trouble with your father for keeping you out so late—and the Mallory woman, too," her aunt said.

"I wish I was as brave as you. I cannot imagine calling Mrs. Mallory by such a name," Molly said, as she put on her coat and took her aunt's hand, the box of treasures stowed safely under her arm.

"One day, Molly, you will realise that age is no reason for respect, and that a child can be far wiser than a grown man or woman. Mrs. Mallory does not deserve our respect. She is a cruel and heartless woman without an ounce of Christian charity in her. But sadly, it would be prudent for you to remain on agreeable terms with her, even if it is painful to do so," her aunt replied.

They walked together across the garden and down the lane leading back to Wisgate Grange. Only a single light burned in a window on the ground floor—Molly's father's study—and they could slip into the house unnoticed, taking the box up to Molly's nursery and hiding it under the bed.

"I will keep it secret," Molly promised, and her aunt nodded.

"It would be wise to do so. Your father would not approve of my filling your head with such ideas. Come now, we shall return downstairs," she said, hurrying Molly out of the nursery and back down to the hallway.

As they came down the stairs, the light of a candle appeared from the kitchen corridor, and the figure of Mrs. Mallory entered the hallway.

"A little late to be creeping about the house, Mrs. Fletcher," she said, a scowl coming over her face.

"If anyone is creeping about the house, Mrs. Mallory, it is you. I have just brought Molly home from the church hall. We have had a delightful evening, as have the servants," she said, and Mrs. Mallory grimaced and shook her head.

"They came back several hours ago, full of boisterousness—a fire eater, I ask you," she replied.

"I thought it was wonderful," Molly said, and her aunt smiled.

"As did I. Now, you must go to bed, Molly. Mrs. Mallory will be eager to lock up, I am sure. Goodnight, my darling," she said, and she leaned down to kiss Molly on the cheek.

"Thank you," Molly whispered.

"Never forget your dreams," her aunt replied, placing a gentle hand on Molly's cheek, and smiling.

Molly watched her leave, Mrs. Mallory's hand now firmly on her shoulder, and when her aunt was out of sight, she tutted and cuffed Molly across the back of her head.

"You wicked child—staying out for all hours. Your aunt is a terrible influence on you," she declared, but Molly only looked up and smiled.

The evening had been perfect, and not even Mrs. Mallory's cruel hand could take away the delight she felt at all she had seen.

"Actually, I think her to be the very best aunt in all the world," she replied, even as Mrs. Mallory's eyes grew wide with anger and she raised her hand to strike Molly once again.

Chapter 4
Practise Makes Perfect

"*Oh... I must be able to make three, just one more try,*" Molly told herself, leaning over her bed in the nursery to fish out the juggling ball which had flown and lodged itself in the gap beneath the window.

She had been practicing her juggling for most of the morning, but try as she might, that third ball eluded her. Anyone could juggle with two–but to add the third ball created such a lack of co-ordination as to make her feel quite giddy. After taking a deep breath, she stood in the middle of the room and threw the balls up into the air for the umpteenth time that morning. They were brightly coloured and filled with rice or some other soft grain, and Molly caught first one, then the next, then the next, passing them upwards–one, two...

"*I will never get the hang of this,*" she chastised herself, sitting down on the floor as the balls fell down next to her with a thud.

She put her head in her hands and sighed, thinking back to the performance the evening before. There, the jugglers had made it look effortless, even passing the juggling balls between themselves, and keeping four or five in the air at once. She pictured herself doing the same, performing on stage with shouts and cheers of applause from an adoring audience.

"Though I would settle with Aunt Sally," she said out loud, thinking back to her aunt's promise of their own dancehall performance at Rosedene.

She picked up the juggling balls, ready to try again. This time, she closed her eyes, picturing their rhythmic movement in the hands of the dancehall performers, and now she threw her own up in the air, opening her eyes and trying not to think too hard about what she was doing. To her amazement, she found she could do it–the balls passing between her hands, one, two, three, and around. A smile came over her face and she laughed, throwing the balls higher into the air. One, two... smash! Molly's eyes grew wide with horror, and she stared at the broken window, through which one of the juggling balls had crashed with such force as to cause the whole pane to shatter. Footsteps now came on the stairs, and Mrs. Mallory's angry cry echoed through the nursery.

"You wicked child! What have you done? What is the meaning of this? When your father discovers what you have done, he will beat you black and blue," she exclaimed, grabbing hold of Molly by the hand and striking her across the cheek.

The sound of the baby crying now came from across the hallway and Mrs. Mallory gave an exasperated cry, calling out for the wet nurse to tend to the screaming infant. The commotion brought Molly's father upstairs, and he appeared in the nursery with a face like thunder, holding the juggling ball in his hand.

"What is this, Molly?" he exclaimed, assuming her guilt before even finding out the facts.

"Please, I was only practicing. Aunt Sally gave me the juggling balls. We are to have a dancehall, you see..." Sally stammered, trembling at the sight of her father's rage.

"A dancehall? Juggling balls? I have never heard such nonsense," he cried, and he leaned down and picked up the other two balls and threw all three of them out of the shattered window.

Molly was glad she had hidden the box containing her aunt's other treasures under the bed, as now her father grabbed her from Mrs. Mallory's hands and shook her, the veins in his neck standing up, his eyes wide with anger.

"I am sorry, Father... I only wanted to practise. I enjoyed seeing the jugglers at the dancehall," she said, fighting back the tears which were welling up in her eyes.

"There will be no more talk of this, Molly—no more of this nonsense. You are nothing but trouble. Do you realise how angry you have made me? Enough!" he cried, and he threw her back on the bed before storming out of the nursery as Mrs. Mallory shook her head.

"We should send you away. No one wants you. You are a nasty, disobedient, and wicked child," she said, tutting as Molly sobbed.

She left the nursery, slamming the door behind her and turning the key in the lock. Molly was left alone, and she wiped the tears from her eyes and sat up, still trembling with fear at what had happened. She had never seen her father so angry with her—he hated her, of that, she was certain, and now she pulled the box from under the bed, opening it to see the treasures her aunt had trusted her with. It comforted her to see them, and she smiled through her tears, taking out the makeup, the funny masks, and magic tricks, imagining the pleasure and delight her aunt had gained from it.

"One day, I shall perform," she whispered, and holding onto that dream, she resolved to do all she could to make it come true.

***

"It was only a matter of time," Molly's aunt said, after Molly had recounted what had happened in the nursery the day before.

"I was only practicing. But I have never seen father so angry, and Mrs. Mallory, too. It was as though they hated me even more than they already did," Molly replied, shaking her head sadly.

"My poor darling, no child your age should feel like that. I wish your father would allow you to come and live here with me. I could speak with him—but I do not think it would do any good. He is… a cruel man, and he is my brother. It is not something one says lightly about one's kin. And Mrs. Mallory, too—a cruel woman, that much is certain," her aunt replied.

"And I lost your juggling balls. Father threw them out of the window into the shrubbery," Molly said, feeling as though she had let her aunt down terribly.

But her aunt smiled at her and rose from her place at the table. They had been taking tea in the parlour at Rosedene, and Molly had been glad of the chance to unburden herself from her troubles. She was an old head on young shoulders, a child already too aware of the sorrowful way in which the world could behave, a fact made worse by that behaviour coming from those who should have loved her most of all.

"And I found them," her aunt replied, reaching into a bag and pulling them out triumphantly.

"But… how? You did not know they were lost," Molly exclaimed, a look of delight coming over her face.

"I was in the garden. Your father does not know that I often go there to collect plants and seeds. I was taking cuttings of a beautiful rhododendron—not that your father cares anything for the garden—and I heard the smash of the window, and then saw the other balls thrown out, too. It was easy to guess what had happened," she said, passing the juggling balls to Molly, who beamed at her in delight.

"Oh… thank you, Aunt Sally. But I cannot take them home with me—if father finds them again, he will…" she began, her words trailing off, not wishing to imagine what her father might do if the decision was his.

"You will keep them here. And practise here. I should have known your father would react in this cruel and uncharitable manner. We must give him no further cause for anger, Molly. He is a volatile man, and prone to the most terrible outbursts of anger. I do not want you in danger—either from him, or the Mallory woman," her aunt replied.

Molly liked to hear her aunt speak of the housekeeper in such a way. Her aunt was afraid of no one, and she imagined her now on one of her adventures into the depths of the jungle in such of her precious butterflies.

"You and my father are so very different," she said, and her aunt laughed.

"Your father has forgotten what it is to be… to laugh, to find joy in simple things. It is a terrible thing to say, but he has become bitter and self-interested. He cared only for a son to inherit his wealth and our poor brother's title–it seems he has that now. It matters not how he treats anyone else–you, or I, or anyone," she said, shaking her head.

Molly watched as her aunt pulled out a handkerchief and dabbed at her eyes. She sighed and beckoned Molly into her embrace.

"But we have one another, Aunt Sally," Molly replied, and her aunt nodded.

"We do, and how thankful I am for that," she said, kissing Molly on the forehead.

***

"Roll up, roll up for a magical, musical, spectacular," Molly called out, addressing the empty garden in a loud voice.

She and her aunt had set up a small stage using upturned packing cases under the shade of the willow tree, and Molly had made a coloured paper banner to string between the trees. They had brought out every chair in the house–even though there was no one to sit on them–and they had laid a table with refreshments–a jug of lemonade and plates of cream cakes, scones, and sandwiches. A banner above the stage, hanging from a branch of the tree, read: "Molly's Music Hall" painted in large red letters, and any observer would have smiled at the sight of the delightful scene before them.

"I think it will be a sell-out performance," her aunt exclaimed, clapping her hands together.

They had even produced a running order, which Molly had meticulously copied several times over in crayon and which listed the acts which were to perform. First would be Molly herself, juggling–her skills now vastly improved–and reciting a poem. Next, her aunt was to sing a song and play the piano, which at great labour they had wheeled out into the garden with the help of a passing boy from the village. Other acts included a display of magic–Molly having learned several ingenious tricks–and an appearance by her aunt's cat pressed into service as a tame lion. A real one having been beyond even Molly's aunt's powers of acquisition.

"We must wait until the appointed hour," Molly said, examining the running order which listed the first performance as scheduled for two O'clock.

"I have not had this much fun in years," her aunt exclaimed, beaming at Molly, as she came to sit on an armchair at the front of the row of chairs.

"I only wish we had a real audience, though I suppose the puppets look real enough," Molly said, glancing at the row of rather odd-looking figures they had sat on various chairs and which her aunt had brought down from the attic, some of whose faces appeared astonishingly life like.

"They had all been made to talk in the past. Perhaps they will come alive for us again today," her aunt replied, picking up one puppet and thrusting her hand up into its skirts.

"Do they really talk?" Molly asked, and her aunt smiled, as from the puppet's mouth there came a voice.

"Do I talk, Molly? Oh, yes, I talk, and I would like to be your friend," the puppet said, in a high-pitched voice, and Molly gave a squeal of delight.

"How did you do that? Your lips did not even move!" she exclaimed, staring at her aunt.

"My lips moved," the puppet said, sounding indignant, opening and shutting its mouth as it spoke.

"But..." Molly said, and she giggled uncontrollably.

"Well, I do not know what is so funny about my talking to you, Molly Walden. All I did was open my mouth to say good day to you and you are in fits of laughter," the puppet exclaimed.

"Oh... I am sorry, it is just–we were not expecting an audience," Molly said, shaking with laughter, her face flushed red, as the puppet now tilted its head to one side.

"I would like to stay–I came here especially from... Timbuktu," the puppet said, and Molly gasped for breath, almost falling off the chair in her delight.

"Then... you are very welcome, but what is your name?" she asked.

The puppet now raised its eyebrows with a click, causing further laughter on Molly's part, before tutting and shaking its head.

"My name is King Leopold, the Third of the kingdom of the giants, but you can call me Clive," it said, and Molly held out her hand for the puppet to shake.

"It is a pleasure to meet you," she said, still trying hard not to laugh.

"And you, Molly Walden," the puppet replied, effecting a low bow.

The conversation continued in this way for some time, and Molly quite forgot it was her aunt who was controlling the puppet's motions and speaking on its behalf. It was a quite remarkable skill, one which Molly was now resolved to learn for herself, and she told her aunt as much when at last Clive settled down to watch the performance.

"But you spoke for him, yet your lips did not move," she said, shaking her head in disbelief.

"The art of the ventriloquist. People have been throwing their voices for many hundreds of years. One does not have to open one's mouth to talk," her aunt said, and Molly smiled.

"I want to learn. I want to learn it all," she replied.

"And you shall—with practise. But look, it is nearly two o'clock," her aunt said, pointing to the clock they had brought out to place on the refreshment table.

Molly hurried to take her place on the stage, glancing at Clive, who was sitting in a wicker chair, perched on a cushion. She could hardly look at him without laughing, and now she took up her juggling balls, as her aunt came to sit on the large armchair in front of the stage.

"Shall I heckle from the stalls, or would you prefer me to behave as an usher shushing the rowdy revellers?" her aunt asked.

"Just applause," Molly said, her three juggling balls in hand, and her aunt dutifully clapped.

Molly closed her eyes. She found this was the best way to begin her act. She would picture the real performers on the stage, throwing the juggling balls to one another and leaping up in the air as they did so. To think of them made her task seem easy, and she tossed the first ball up into the air, followed by the second, and then the third, opening her eyes as her hands now followed their rhythm of the passing balls, back and forth in an arc. Her aunt applauded furiously.

"Oh, bravo, Molly. I did not know your skills were so advanced–you have been practicing hard," she exclaimed.

Molly made no reply, her entire concentration on the circling balls, as now she threw them higher, stepping from foot to foot, back and forth, smiling at the thought of her aunt's amazement. She had been practicing–very hard–and she was proud of her achievements.

"And I thank you," she said, catching the three balls and taking a bow as her aunt leaped to her feet.

They had picked roses from the garden and her aunt now threw several stems onto the stage as though they were at the finale of an opera in a grand European theatre.

"Marvellous, you were simply marvellous. I would never have believed you had such skills, Molly," she exclaimed.

"I really did practise very hard," Molly said, and her aunt nodded, stepping up onto the stage next to her.

"And practise will make perfect. Now, you must take your seat and I shall sing to you," she said, and Molly smiled, hurrying down to sit next to Clive on a small wooden stool as her aunt cleared her throat.

"Is it the one about the spring flowers?" Molly asked, and her aunt nodded.

"They very one—and to sing it in the garden seems entirely appropriate—we shall sing it to the flowers," she replied, and taking a deep breath, she sang.

***

The dancehall performances went on for most of the afternoon. Molly clapped and cheered as her aunt sang and danced on the stage, before taking her place at the piano and playing a tune which she had written herself. Next came Molly's turn again, and she performed several magic tricks, culminating in removing a silver coin from Clive's mouth, her sleight of hand well-practised. They recited poetry, sang songs, and brought the cat, named Marjorie, onto the stage for the finale.

"Oh, do stay still, Marjorie," Molly said, trying to get the cat to sit so that she might shower her with rose petals in a final flourishing magic trick.

But Marjorie was having none of it and she scampered off the stage and into the shrubbery, still wearing the pink bonnet which Molly had somehow tied over her head.

"You will not get her to sit still, Molly. I think the performance is over. But what fun we have had," her aunt said, stepping up onto the stage and taking Molly by the hand.

"We must bow now," Molly said, and the two of them gave a low bow, as Molly imagined Clive and the other puppets applauding them.

"And one day, perhaps you will be on a proper stage, Molly, and have a real audience – rather than just Clive and his friends," her aunt said, smiling at Molly, who nodded.

"I really hope so. If I practise really hard, do you think it's possible?" she asked, and her aunt nodded.

"I think all dreams are possible... we only have to want them enough," she replied, putting her arm around Molly, and kissing her on the forehead.

Part Two

Chapter 5
The Last Act

"I want it!" Tobias exclaimed, snatching the book out of Molly's hands as she sat reading on the window seat in the nursery.

He was five now, and Molly was twelve, but whilst Molly had grown into a kinder and more thoughtful girl, her brother had grown into the very opposite. Even at the tender age of five, he knew himself the favoured one, spoiled and feted in equal measure, constantly reminded of his status as the apple of his father's eye—the inheritance of the Barony all but certain. He was an ugly-looking child, his face pale, his brown eyes large, his dark hair matted, his features gaunt—the very opposite of his pretty sister whom he took delight in taunting whenever the opportunity arose.

"I am reading it at the moment, Tobias—I will read it to you if you wish," Molly said, but Tobias wanted it for himself.

She had learned to be a model of patience in dealing with her brother's moods. It was not his fault he had been raised in such a way, even if his behaviour tested her to the limits.

"It is mine. I will tell Father. He will take it off you," Tobias cried, and he struck out at Molly, beating her with his little fists.

It was no use arguing. Tobias was right. Her father would take the book off her and give it to her brother. He always took his side in any dispute, and this would be no different. Whatever the perceived injustice, it would be Tobias who would be in the right, and Molly who would be in the wrong. That was how things were at Wisgate Grange, and Molly had grown used to it. With a sigh, she handed the book to Tobias, rising to her feet and doing the only thing which she knew would placate the situation—leaving.

"I hope you will enjoy it, Tobias," she said, as Tobias tossed it aside in favour of another, more interesting, toy.

He ignored her, rolling on his back and screaming—his way of gaining attention—and Molly slipped out of the nursery, knowing her father would blame her for his tantrum. She slipped down the back stairs to the kitchen, avoiding Mrs. Mallory, who was chastising one housemaid for the appalling state of the brass, and out into the garden. She was going to see her aunt, and she picked a bunch of primroses from the grassy bank which rose to the trees which bordered the lawn, before making her way through the gate and out into the lane which led to Rosedene. It was a sunny day, wisps of white cloud trailing across the blue sky above, and the sun warm on her neck. Molly smiled to herself—her brother would cause havoc for Mrs. Mallory, and her father would start shouting at the top of his voice. But out here, all was calm, and Molly breathed a deep sigh as she came to her aunt's gate, the scent of the garden wafting over her.

"What beautiful flowers, Molly," her aunt exclaimed, as Molly presented them to her a few moments later.

"I picked them just a short while ago. They will look lovely in your green vase," Molly said, running to fetch a jug of water, as her aunt placed the flowers in the empty vase on the table.

She had been busy cataloguing several new species of butterfly, and Molly looked down at the wingspans in fascination, never ceasing to be amazed by her aunt's remarkable interest.

"These are moths, Molly—but they are unusual in that they have such vivid colouring to the wingspan. I had to set up a lamp in the garden and wait for several hours before I attracted them. It is the plants, you see—the right mix of plants will bring the right butterflies and moths you desire. That is why a knowledge of plants goes hand in hand with the butterfly collector's art. Whenever I visited a new place, I would learn of its flora and fauna first before setting about catching the butterflies," her aunt said, as Molly returned with a jug of water.

"I would like to learn more about them—but Tobias snatched the book you gave me the other day. I fear he may have already torn the pages," she said, and her aunt tutted.

"That child is a... a tearaway," she exclaimed.

Molly knew her aunt had no love for Tobias—she showed it well enough on her visits to Wisgate Grange—and, in return, Molly's father had become crueller in his attitude towards Molly herself. It was a cruel game, one in which there could be no winners, only a loser—Molly.

"And forever indulged. He is not scolded or chastised, and they never speak an angry word against him. It is always I who am to blame for his behaviour," Molly said, looking at the primroses now displayed in the vase.

"Well... cast such thoughts aside, Molly. You need not think about him anymore now. Your father and he are well suited to one another. I am sorry to say that Tobias will grow up believing everything he demands he receives, and it will be a sorry lesson when he learns the opposite," her aunt replied.

Molly nodded. It was the truth, and she knew there could be no escaping the sad fact of Tobias' future—like father, like son. She turned her attention now to the moths laid out on her aunt's workbench. One was bigger than her hand, its wings appearing gilded with silver, and symmetrical patterns arched in a crescent on each of its wingspans. She marvelled at it, peering down at eye level with the creature who might well still been alive if Molly had not known better.

"Do they feel pain?" Molly asked, looking up at her aunt, who shook her head.

"I do not believe so—not in a conventional sense, at least. The shock of being caught creates a paralysis—they are stunned, and it is only a matter of moments before they are put beyond pain all together. I would not worry about it, Molly," she said, and Molly nodded.

"There is so much to learn," she said, turning her attentions to the glass cabinets.

She knew all her aunt's specimens. They were catalogued perfectly, each one labelled and recorded in the ledgers lining the walls of the parlour. The newest case lay beneath the window, and Molly's aunt now took the moth from her workbench and laid it carefully in the case, pinning down the wings with small hair pins, barely visible to the naked eye.

"I treated the moth with a preservative. It will long outlive either you or I," she said, closing the glass lid of the case.

"Will people look at them in years to come?" Molly asked, fascinated at the thought of future generations marvelling at her aunt's collection.

"This is a noble pursuit, Molly—the pursuit of the scientist. We are making discoveries all the time and contributing in our own way to an understanding of the world. Have I not always told you that the most important thing is to follow one's dreams? I am glad to have done that in my life, and I pray you shall do the same in yours," her aunt said.

Molly had but one dream—to be a performer, to have a real audience, and to hear the cries of delight from those who came to witness the spectacle of her act. She thought about it often, longing for a chance to prove her long hours of practise in an actual performance. Her aunt was very kind with her compliments, but ever since the night she had watched in awe at the dancehall troupe's show, Molly had desired to stand alongside them and hear the roar of an audience in her ears.

"I do not know how I will ever do so. The dancehall has never returned, and even if it does, how will I prove myself to them?" she asked, a forlorn note entering her voice.

Her aunt looked at her and raised her eyebrows.

"We should not think too carefully about how things will be accomplished–only that they will be. Opportunity is usually the most reliable source of fortune," she said.

Molly smiled. Her aunt had a way of making things sound possible, reasonable, and within her grasp. She glanced for a last time at the moth in the display case, returning to the table and sitting down. Her aunt went to make tea, returning with a large tray on which were a silver-plated teapot, two China cups and saucers, and a large sugar bowl with tongs for the cubes which were piled up like blocks of ice into a precarious mountain.

"You always cheer me up, Aunt Sally–I wish I could live here all the time," Molly said.

"As do I, my dear... oh, the cake!" she exclaimed, and she set the tray down and turned to hurry back to the kitchen.

But as she did so, she clutched at her side and winced, coughing violently, and pulling out her handkerchief. Molly leaped to her feet and rushed to her aunt's side. She was bent double, holding the handkerchief to her mouth.

"Aunt Sally, whatever is the matter?" Molly said, helping her aunt into one of the wicker chairs by the hearth.

Her aunt had turned suddenly pale, her lips blue, her eyes withdrawn. To her horror, Molly saw the handkerchief was stained red with blood.

"I... I do not know, Molly. A fit of some kind, I am sure it will pass," she said, but Molly could hear the fear in her voice.

Her aunt was always the very model of confidence–it was she who so often buoyed Molly up from her sadness, but now… Molly could tell she was afraid, and she put her arms around her, even as her aunt coughed once again.

"I will run for the doctor–he can come at once. We can put you to bed. I will stay–Father cannot object to my remaining here, not if you are ill," Molly said, and she helped her aunt to sit back in her chair as she snatched up her shawl to hurry from the house.

"Molly, you must not trouble the doctor. I will be all right," her aunt said, but Molly was fighting back the tears welling up in her eyes, and she shook her head, refusing to do as she was told.

"I must bring him, Aunt Sally, I cannot…" she began, and unable to finish her sentence, she fled from the parlour and out into the garden.

She had been about to say that she could not bear to lose her aunt as she had her mother. Molly knew too well the signs of sickness her aunt was displaying. The white death, tuberculosis–the paleness of the skin, the terrible cough, the blood—tears welled up in her eyes and she paused, leaning against a tree and look back forlornly at Rosedene. Her hands were trembling, and she shook her head, offering a silent prayer in desperation for the feelings which now welled up inside her. To lose her aunt would be to lose the only friend she had, the only kindness in her life.

"*It cannot be. It will not be,*" she told herself, and she hurried off along the lane towards the village, knowing she must summon the doctor as soon as possible.

***

"Tuberculosis," the doctor said, rising to his feet and glancing back at Molly, who was standing in the doorway of her aunt's bedroom.

Her aunt was lying beneath a patchwork eiderdown, dressed now in her nightgown. Her face was pale, but the trembling had stopped and she coughed only intermittently, thanks to a soothing tonic given her by the doctor–a young man named Wilkins who had been in practise in Wisgate for only a year.

"And there I was imagining some remarkable tropical disease which could be named after me would take me in my youth," Molly's aunt said, even as tears rose in Molly's eyes.

"Do not say such things, Aunt Sally. You have a long life ahead of you–tuberculosis is... it does not mean a death sentence," Molly replied, for she knew that many people of the upper classes lived for many years with the condition, pale and withdrawn, perhaps, but still alive.

"Your aunt must rest, Molly–no more leaping about with butterfly nets, no more exuberances at dancing and singing," Doctor Wilkins said, for he knew well enough the things which occurred at Rosedene between Molly and her aunt.

"Then what is life without such things, Doctor Wilkins? Am I to become like one of my puppets? Lying here, mute and incapable?" Molly's aunt asked.

"Rest is what you need, Mrs. Fletcher, and I am sure your niece will do all she can to ensure you have that rest," the doctor said, raising his eyebrows.

He prescribed a further tonic and reiterated the necessity of rest before bidding them a good day. Molly went over to her aunt's bed and knelt at the side, taking her aunt's hand in hers and kissing it. It felt cold to the touch, and she looked up into her aunt's eyes with a worried expression on her face.

"I... I do not want..." she began, but her aunt stopped her.

"Do not say those words. We both know the sorrow which is to come. The white death is... an end. But I have lived a long and happy life. I have seen things which most people can only dream of, and I have experienced enough for two or three lifetimes over. It is not a cause of sorrow, Molly. Life comes to an end for us all. It is what we have done with that life which matters," her aunt said, taking Molly's hand in hers and squeezing it.

"But... it will not come soon, will it? You will regain your strength for now," Molly replied.

Her aunt sighed and shook her head.

"I do not know, Molly–perhaps I will, perhaps I will not. But I know one thing–I shall have you at my side in all things, and the thought of that makes me extremely happy," she said.

Molly gave a weak smile, but inside, her heart was breaking. She fought back the tears in her eyes, not wishing to show her aunt the genuine sorrow inside her.

"I will do all I can to look after you," she assured her.

"I know you will–and you have been the very best of companions. I see myself in you every day, and that has kept me young, truly, it has," her aunt said.

Molly watched as she closed her eyes. A little colour had now returned to her cheeks, but still had the look of sickness about her. Molly had known other people struck down by the white death–pale women in bath chairs, whom her mother had taken her to visit in stuffy drawing rooms and who lamented the tragedy of their weakness, likening it to a martyrdom. Her aunt would not suffer so, she was strong, and Molly held onto that thought as she returned home that afternoon.

"You are playing tardy, Molly–tea is at four O'clock, it is not twenty minutes after the hour," Mrs. Mallory said, pointing Molly towards the drawing room where her and Tobias's tea would be laid out on a low table.

"I want to speak to Father," Molly said, and Mrs. Mallory raised her eyebrows.

"Your father is busy, and what could you possibly have to say to him?" she demanded, her hand twitching as though she were about to strike Molly for her insolence.

"My Aunt Sally is sick. She has the... white death. That is why I was late coming home. I had to run for Doctor Wilkins. But I must tell Father. He would surely wish to know," Molly said, believing that her aunt's suffering would touch even her father and Mrs. Mallory.

Mrs. Mallory gave a curt nod and pointed towards the study. It was rare for Molly to address her father directly. Usually, she was afraid of him. But a boldness now came over her, and she stepped forward, raising her hand to knock at the door.

"Yes?" her father's voice came from beyond.

"I need to speak with you, Father," Molly replied.

There was a pause, and then footsteps. The door was flung open, and her father peered down at her with an angry expression on his face.

"And what, pray, could be so important as to demand you interrupt me?" he asked.

Molly's hands were trembling, but she cleared her throat and looked up at her father defiantly.

"My aunt is sick–the doctor says it is the white death. I wanted you to know, you may wish to visit her–you should visit her," Molly said.

Her father's face displayed only the slightest hint of shock before he shook his head and waved his hand dismissively.

"She will live yet. A disease like that does not immediately claim life," he said, and Molly's eyes grew wide with tears.

"But she needs us," she exclaimed, her anger rising at her father, who displayed only a callous disregard for what she was saying.

"Is that so? Well, I do not need her," he said, and before Molly could reply, he slammed the study door in her face.

Molly turned to find Mrs. Mallory staring at her, a satisfied expression on her face.

"I knew he would show little concern," she said, pointing towards the drawing room door.

Molly made no answer and made her way across the hall to the drawing room, where she found Tobias greedily devouring cream cakes.

"You were too late. I ate yours," he said, sneering at her with a mouth covered in cake crumbs.

"I am not hungry, Tobias–you eat them, eat them and be happy," she cried, and with that, she fled from the room with tears rolling down her cheeks.

***

"Use them with some force, Molly–you are not giving your brother a haircut," Molly's aunt said, as Molly used a pair of shears to cut back the rhododendrons which had suddenly burst into a riot of foliage and flower in the late spring sunshine.

"It seems a shame to cut them back so vigorously," Molly replied, looking down at the piles of petals and leaves at her feet.

"But that is precisely what you must do to ensure renewed growth next year. A plant like this will only flourish when it is treated harshly. There is a lesson for us all in that–sometimes we must prune ourselves if we are to become something more," her aunt replied.

She was sitting in the bath chair which Molly had wheeled out onto the lawn for her. She had a blanket over her knees–despite the warmth of the day–and her face was pale and gaunt. It had been a month since her diagnosis and whilst the doctor had done all he could to help ease her symptoms, there was no doubt the disease was taking hold. Molly had done all she could for her aunt, and she was hardly ever away from her company at Rosedene, but she had felt a sense of helplessness at what lay ahead. She could plump her cushions, make pots of chicken soup, air the house, and a hundred other things to make life easier, but she could do nothing to cure the sickness which, day by day, was slowly creeping over her aunt, casting its long shadow on every aspect of her life.

"Then I should cut back more?" Molly asked.

"A lot more," her aunt replied, and Molly looked up at the rhododendrons and chopped, bringing down a shower of petals and leaves.

When she had finished, she stepped back, glancing at her aunt, who nodded approvingly.

"But there is hardly anything left," she said.

"Which means the plant puts all its efforts into the lower growth. It becomes strong at the root. There is no point in blossoming if you have not the foundations to sustain it," her aunt remarked.

Molly liked these sayings of her aunt. They were always so filled with wisdom. She could not help but admire her aunt who, even in her time of suffering, found reason to rejoice in simple things such as her garden or her butterfly collection, and who always had a comforting word when Molly was feeling down.

"Then I am to cut all the plants back?" Molly asked, gazing around the garden.

"Cut back and watch them grow—you will find that is the rhythm of any garden. Think of the seasons. Winter does its own pruning and blossoming. Autumn ends the summer, winter kills back the growth, and spring brings life blossoming again. It is the cycle of the seasons which is most important, Molly," her aunt replied.

Molly had set up a table on the lawn and now she hurried inside to fetch a tray of tea things and a cake she had made that morning. But as she returned outside, she heard her aunt coughing violently, and she set the tray down on the grass and hurried across the lawn to where her aunt was sitting in her bath chair.

"Aunt Sally?" Molly exclaimed, and her aunt gasped for breath.

Her face had grown pale, her eyes wide, and she was struggling to breathe. Molly took her hand in hers., trying to reassure her.

"The tonic, Molly–fetch the tonic," her aunt gasped.

Molly ran back inside, returning a few moments later with a large bottle of the tonic Doctor Wilkins had brought with him on his visit the day before, along with a spoon and a glass of water.

"It will be all right, Aunt Sally. Here, take a spoonful," she said, her hands shaking as she poured the liquid from the bottle onto the spoon.

"Oh, I cannot… Molly, it is…" her aunt replied, her voice rasping, and now her eyes grew wider and she sat back in the chair, pushing aside the tonic and knocking the spoon to the ground.

"You do not know what you are saying, Aunt Sally. Please, take the medicine," Molly implored her.

But her aunt was unresponsive. Her face had grown paler, her body seeming to shrink back in the chair, and Molly took hold of her hand, desperately trying to revive her. At that moment, the boy who helped in the garden appeared, and Molly called for him to run and fetch the doctor with immediate haste.

"I will, Miss Walden," he called back, running off along the lane towards the village.

Molly could get no response from her aunt, her skin cold to the touch. Tears were running down her cheeks, and she begged her to wake up, to say something, to open her eyes and tell Molly everything would be all right.

"Aunt Sally? Please wake up," Molly implored her, but the only response was silence...

Chapter 6
A Parting Gift

The doctor could do nothing for Molly's aunt. She had died in the throes of the fever, and no medicine on earth could have saved her. He arrived a short while later, having summoned Molly's father on the way. He came with some reluctance, standing a short distance off as Doctor Wilkins examined the lifeless body of Molly's aunt, lying in the bath chair.

"Sometimes it is a gradual slipping away, and at others, a violent death. Your aunt has been spared the worst, and she is at peace now," the doctor said as Molly stood at his side gazing at her aunt's lifeless body.

"There was nothing I could do," she said, completely in shock at what she had witnessed, and the awful truth she was now confronted with.

"There was nothing anyone could have done, Molly. Your aunt would not wish for you to be upset. She told me herself her time had come. Rejoice in her life. Do not linger over her death," he said, beckoning to the undertakers who had been loitering in the lane, waiting to take the body away.

Molly watched in silence as they lifted her aunt's lifeless body into a simple coffin made of cedar wood. It had a brass cross on the top, and they closed the lid before hoisting it sombrely onto their shoulders. She pulled out a handkerchief and dabbed at the tears rolling down her cheeks. It felt as though she was watching herself from afar, watching as tragedy unfolded, knowing the awful truth of what was to come. She felt entirely alone, devoid of kindness, friendship, and love. Her aunt had meant everything to her, and now she was gone. What more could there be?

"Come now, Molly. Do not stand there like a statue of misery," her father said, striding across the lawn and beckoning her to follow.

"I want to stay here," Molly said, clinging to the last shreds of familiarity.

Rosedene was her home–it was here she had felt happy, and safe. But her father now grabbed her by the arm and pulled her forward, bringing his face to hers. His expression twisted into a snarl.

"Enough of this foolish sentimentality, Molly. Your aunt is dead. There is nothing you can do to bring her back. Perhaps she would have lived longer if she had not been so foolish as to travel to heaven knows where and bring back heaven knows what diseases. She had this coming to her. It was only a matter of time," he snapped.

"But it was the white death–nothing to do with her travels. Why must you be so cruel?" Molly cried, no longer caring for what dreadful punishment her father might exact for such insubordination.

He raised his hand and struck her across the cheek, his face flushed red with anger.

"I will hear no more of this," he exclaimed, and dragging her by the arm, he pulled her roughly through the garden gate, as Molly stared desperately back at Rosedene, the one place she had known happiness, a happiness which now was gone.

***

"Forasmuch as it hath pleased Almighty God of his great mercy to take unto himself the soul of our dear sister here departed. We therefore commit her body to the ground; earth to earth, ashes to ashes, dust to dust; in sure and certain hope of the Resurrection to eternal life, through our Lord Jesus Christ; who shall change our vile body, that it may be like unto his glorious body, according to the mighty working, whereby he is able to subdue all things to himself," the curate, Mr. Crockford, said, casting down a shower of earth into the grave, before stepping back so that Molly and her cousin, Harold, might do the same.

The funeral of Molly's aunt was taking place a week after her death. With her wishes, it was a simple affair. The ceremonies at the graveside followed a short service in the church. Only Molly and Harold stood as the principal mourners, joined by some from the village who had known Molly's aunt after her return from abroad. Molly's father was notable by his absence, having claimed he had no wish to search for the living amongst the dead. The grave lay next to that of Molly's mother, in the plot belonging to the Walden family and in which many of Molly's ancestors were buried.

"Thank you, Mr. Crockford," Molly said when the prayers had concluded, and they had stepped back to allow the gravedigger to fill in the grave.

"I admired your aunt a great deal–she had some remarkable stories to tell. A quite astonishing woman, by all accounts," he said, patting Molly on the shoulder.

Her cousin, Harold, the Baronet Wisgate, was some years older than she, and it had been several years since last she had seen him. He was a recluse and sickly young man and looked thoroughly uncomfortable at having been removed from the seclusion of his study, if only for a few hours of necessary duty as titular head of the family. He was dressed in a long, grey overcoat, with a black tie at his neck and a tall top hat on his head.

"She will leave it to you," he remarked, and Molly looked at him in surprise.

"What do you mean?" she asked.

"Rosedene, of course. The house, the butterfly collection, all of it," he said, and Molly shook her head, brushing away the tears from her eyes.

"Why would she leave it to me? I do not want it. I only want her back," she said, and not waiting for Harold to respond, she turned on her heels and hurried off across the churchyard.

She had barely been able to watch as they had lowered the coffin into the ground, caught up in thoughts of her own sad predicament. Her only friend was gone, and with her, all hope for the future. Molly had wept for a week, but her father had been right about one thing–no amount of sorrow would bring her aunt back. There was nothing which could be done save remember her and rejoice in the happiness she had brought. It was this thought which Molly clung to as she walked back to Wisgate Grange that afternoon, enduring the sympathies of well-meaning people on the way.

"Your aunt was a good woman, Miss Walden," one of the farmer's wives said, whilst another stopped Molly to tell her a story of her aunt once giving her a shilling so that she might visit her son in the military hospital in Bath.

"As good a soul as an could wish for," she said.

It cheered Molly a little to hear her aunt spoken of in such terms, even if no amount of kindly sentiment could bring her back. But when she arrived home, she found Mrs. Mallory waiting for her, and any sense of cheer in the memory of her aunt's good deeds was swiftly cast aside.

"Your father wants to see you, Molly. He is in his study. Go to him," she snapped.

Molly caught sight of Tobias peering around the drawing room door, his face contorted into an unpleasant sneer.

"You are in trouble," he said, sounding gleeful.

Mrs. Mallory pointed to the study door, and Molly took a deep breath and approached. She was still wearing her black shawl and mourning dress, a veil pulled down over her eyes, and she knocked, waiting for her father to respond.

"Enter," he called out, and Molly opened the door, surprised to find her father in the company of an elderly gentleman she did not recognise.

He had on a black frock coat and tails, and a pair of half-moon spectacles perched on the end of his enormous nose. His face was red, and his whiskers stuck out at odd angles, giving him a most peculiar look.

"Ah, this is the girl, is it?" he said, his voice high-pitched and squeaking.

"This is her, yes," Molly's father said, as the man stepped forward to examine her.

"She has her mother's likeness, though I can see your own mother in her, too, my Lord," the man said.

Molly's father looked up and raised his eyebrows.

"You did not come here to speak of family resemblance, Mr. Coutts, sir. Get on with the business in hand," he said, and the man flushed even redder than he already was and cleared his throat.

"Yes, of course. Forgive me. You will not know who I am, Molly, and why should you, but my name is Mr. Arthur Coutts, of Coutts and Bainbridge, we are your father's– your family's–solicitors and we are dealing with the process of your aunt's will," he said.

Molly stared at him in wide-eyed disbelief. Her aunt was not yet cold in the grave and already discussion had turned to her will. She shook her head and stepped back, tears welling up in her eyes, as she stammered her response.

"I... I have only just returned from the funeral. We have only just laid my aunt to rest," she said, glancing at her father hoping to shame him into a response.

"Ah… yes, well… it seems pertinent then to discuss the contents of the will with you," he began, but Molly's father interrupted him.

"Just get on with it, Coutts. Tell her what it says," he exclaimed, banging his fist down hard on his desk.

"Well… to put it simply, Miss Walden, you are your aunt's sole inheritor. Rosedene, her collections of butterflies and books, the small income she had from the estate—all of it is yours. When you come of age, that is," he said, and Molly stared up at him in wide-eyed amazement.

Her aunt had never made mention of her will. Molly had never given thought to the possibility of what would happen should her aunt die—it was not something she had wished to dwell on. But it made perfect sense, too. Her aunt and her father had never got on, and Molly's aunt had always known of the cruel manner in which she was treated.

"She left it all to me?" Molly said, and the solicitor nodded.

"Down to the last penny—but not until you come of age. You cannot simply move into Rosedene tomorrow," he said, laughing at his own joke.

"It will be contested," her father said, his tone sounding dark and threatening.

"But… my Lord, there is really nothing to contest. I was present when your sister made the will—I am one of its witnesses, along with my business partner, Mr. Bainbridge. We both of us knew of your sister's wishes. She was adamant that the property and what small legacy was hers should go to Molly," he said, glancing nervously at Molly, who took a deep breath and folded her arms.

"I know it is what she wanted—that is why she taught me to take care of the garden and the butterfly collection. She was... preparing me," Molly replied.

At these words, her father leapt to his feet and banged both his fists down on the table, his face flushed red with anger.

"Enough! I will hear no more about it. Do as you must do, Mr. Coutts, but there will be no more talk of Molly's inheritance. I refuse to accept it," he snarled.

"Very good, my Lord. I shall see myself out," the solicitor said, offering Molly's father a curt bow before patting Molly on the shoulder and letting himself out of the study.

"Why do you not want me to have Rosedene, Father?" Molly asked, for she could think of no reason other than her father's unnecessary cruelty for his vehement opposition to her aunt's wishes.

"What right have you to demand such an answer from me?" he said, as he came to the other side of the desk and stood towering over her.

"Because I do not understand your opposition, your lack of love. Why do you hate me so much?" she demanded, fighting back the tears which were welling up in her eyes.

"Hate you? I never wanted you, Molly—I never wanted you so as to hate you. Now get out," he cried, pointing a trembling hand at the door.

Molly fled. She slammed the door behind her, pushing past Mrs. Mallory, who had been listening at the keyhole. Tobias was standing in the middle of the hallway, a gloating look on his little face, and he made a grab for her as she ran past.

"You stop, I demand it," he exclaimed, but Molly now turned to him, shaking her head as tears rolled down her cheeks.

"You will be just like him, Tobias—filled with hate and all that is bad. I want nothing to do with you—with any of you," she exclaimed, and before Mrs. Mallory could stop her, she had fled the house, not stopping until she arrived at the gate into the garden of Rosedene.

Even after just a week, the garden was becoming overgrown. The rhododendrons which she and her aunt had cut back the week before were sprouting new growth and the grass was growing thick and lush. Flowers were blooming in the beds, and a sweet, perfumed scent hung in the air. The death of Molly's aunt had, like the end of winter, brought forth the blossoming of spring. Molly sat down beneath the boughs of the weeping willow, hidden by its long, drooping branches. She had stopped crying now, for in the garden, she felt cradled by the happy memories of her aunt and all they had shared.

"And now it is mine," she said to herself, unable to believe her aunt's kindness in leaving Rosedene and all its treasures to her as a legacy.

It took a while before she plucked up the courage to enter the house. Her aunt had always kept a key hidden beneath a large pot to the left of the door, and Molly turned it in the lock, letting herself into the parlour, which was exactly as her aunt had left it. On the table, several volumes lay open with pictures of exotic butterflies gazing up from the pages, and the remnants of the tea which she and Molly had taken on the day of her death stood on a tray in the kitchen, and which Molly had brought inside when the doctor had arrived. It was like a moment in time, frozen, and Molly stood staring silently around her at the scene.

"And now it is all mine," she thought to herself.

She was only twelve years old, but she could feel the burden of responsibility weighing heavily on her—the burden of her aunt's legacy and all she had taught her. She examined the room, wondering if her aunt had left anything which might explain this strange and unexpected set of circumstances. Her sorrow was lifted in this way, for being in the parlour of Rosedene made her feel close to her aunt, a closeness she found comforting. Everything there was familiar—the paintings, the books, the butterfly collection. All of it spoke of the woman whom Molly had loved more than anyone else in all the world.

"What treasures," she exclaimed, pulling open a draw to reveal a set of remarkable carved stones, covered in strange symbols—souvenirs of one of her aunt's many trips abroad.

She continued to explore the house, marvelling at the things she found there. Her aunt's bedroom was the last place she arrived at and she stood in the doorway, looking at the neatly made bed and the shelves of books which lined the walls. But it was a newspaper, folded on the bedside table, which drew her attention, and on which her aunt had drawn a circle in pencil around an advertisement. She went over and picked it up, peering at the date which was marked as eight days previously—the day before she had died. A smile now came over Molly's face as she gazed down at the circled advertisement.

"Roll up, roll up for the spectacular extravaganza of Algernon Trott's Travelling Dancehall
Appearing for one night only in Wisgate, Bedfordshire
Wednesday 4th July at six O'clock in the church hall
Jugglers, magicians, & and the remarkable
Mr. Mar volo!"

A tear rolled down Molly's cheek as she realised this was the message her aunt had left her. She had wanted her to find this, to share the news which Molly had so long been waiting for—the return of the dancehall troupe and the chance to see her dreams made real again. How tragic it was that her aunt was not alive to see this. They would have gone together and perhaps they would even have performed together, to the delight of the crowds. But Molly knew what she had to do—she had to go to the performance and see where her dreams would lead her.

"I shall do this for you, Aunt Sally," she said, sitting down on the bed where the scent of her aunt's perfume remained, and with a sense of excitement coming over her, Molly gazed down at the advertisement once more, imagining the delights which were to come.

Chapter 7
A Decision Made

"And they say he eats fire—breathes it out, just like a dragon," the housemaid was saying, as Molly entered the dining room the next morning.

She had taken the newspaper advertisement with her from Rosedene the evening before, but the coming of the dancehall that very week was the talk of the village. Molly had been so wrapped up in her grief and the preparations for the funeral that she had barely noticed life going on as normal around her.

"We will have none of that foolish talk, Lucy. See to your chores," Mrs. Mallory snapped, scowling at Molly, who now took her place at the table.

Tobias was sitting at the head of the table eating a piece of toasted bread, crunching on it loudly, and he looked at Molly with a disdainful expression on his face. A five-year-old child should never have been so certain of his own superiority, but Tobias had been taught the fact of that superiority from the earliest of ages, and Molly was under no illusion that he would not grow into an ever more unpleasant individual as the years went by.

"I do not want to go," he announced, and Molly raised her eyebrows at him, knowing he was only saying as much to ingratiate himself with the housekeeper.

"And quite right, my Lord," Mrs. Mallory said, beaming at him.

"I think it is silly–clowns and magicians and animals parading around," he said, looking at Molly hoping to gain a reaction from her.

"No one is asking you to go," Molly replied, reaching out for a piece of toasted bread.

"Do not speak so rudely to your brother," Mrs. Mallory said.

"*She* will want to go. My aunt filled her head with silly ideas – that is what Father says," Tobias continued.

Molly now saw what he was to become–his tone of voice, his mannerisms, his entire demeanour, was just like that of their father. It made her shudder to see it.

"And what if I wish to go?" Molly retorted, the anger rising in her at the injustice of her brother's words–who was he to speak for their father, even if Molly knew he was right?

"You will not be going, Molly. There is no one to take you. It was your aunt who encouraged that foolishness and look what it led to," Mrs. Mallory said, for she had never forgotten the smashed window and the missing juggling balls.

"I can go by myself," Molly replied, but Mrs. Mallory only laughed.

"You will go nowhere, Molly. Not unless your father agrees and he will not," she replied, taking up a tray of breakfast things and leaving the room.

"You cannot go. Father will forbid it," Tobias said, his face etched with glee.

"Why must you be such a horrible child?" Molly asked, but her brother only sneered at her.

"And why must I have a sister at all? No one wants you, Molly," he replied, and jumping down from his chair, he ran past her, pulling her hair as he did so.

Molly sighed, trying her best not to allow the tears to well up in her eyes. But Tobias's words—and the threat of Mrs. Mallory—had only heightened her resolve. She would attend the performance come what may, and later that morning she sought Lucy, the housemaid who had spoken with such excitement about the dancehall, hoping she would help her with her plan.

"I remember the last performance, Miss Molly—it was such a delight. I was not very old, just eleven, but I have dreamed of it ever since," Lucy said.

She was a young girl, only just seventeen years old, with a pretty face and strawberry blonde hair neatly tied back. She was making up one of the beds when Molly approached her, and she gave her a sympathetic look as Molly explained her predicament.

"I dearly wish to go. It means more to me than anything, but I know my father will forbid it," Molly said, sitting on the floor with a heavy sigh.

"It is not right, Miss Molly—the way you are treated. I see the way Mrs. Mallory looks at you. We all do. But there is none of us brave enough to speak out in your defence. I am sorry, Miss Molly," Lucy said, shaking her head.

"But if I gave you the money, you could buy a ticket for me—and for yourself. My aunt has left me Rosedene, you see, and there is money, too—an allowance, but also a sum she had hidden in the house. I can give you it now," Molly said, rummaging in her pocket and bringing out the coins she had stowed there for just this hope.

Lucy looked at her with a worried expression on her face.

"But suppose your father discovers you have been there? What then?" she asked.

"I will not be here to suffer the consequences," Molly replied, and the maid stared at her with wide-eyed astonishment.

"But… what do you mean?" she asked, furrowing her brow.

Molly took a deep breath. She had been thinking long and hard about the matter and had made her mind up. She intended to run away. It seemed a simple matter in her mind. She would prepare a few simple things—clothes, a little food, some money—and slip away during the night when the dancehall troupe left Wisgate for their next destination. It had always been her dream to join them, and now was her chance—perhaps the only chance she would ever have. She knew her plan was dangerous, and that discovery would mean only further untold punishment, but it was a risk she had to take. There was something drawing her on, a spark of adventure ignited by the sorrowfulness of her current predicament. She thought of her aunt and what she would say if she had known Molly's intentions.

"Always follow your dreams, Molly," she would say, and it was that dream which Molly intended to follow.

"I mean, I am leaving Wisgate Grange, I am going to run away," Molly replied, and Lucy gasped.

"But–oh, you should not have told me, Miss Molly. I–we will be so worried about you," she said, throwing her arms around Molly and pulling her into an embrace.

Molly knew the servants hated to see her treated so badly–it was for that reason she had trusted Lucy with the secret. But to remain in Wisgate was a suffering she knew she could not endure any longer, not without her aunt, who had been her only source of happiness.

"I made my mind up. I need you to buy the ticket for me and to leave the side door unlocked after Mrs. Mallory has retired to her sitting room for the evening. I will slip out at dusk and see the performance, then… well, I do not entirely know. All I know is that I must get as far away from this terrible place as possible," she said, and Lucy looked at her with tears in her eyes.

"Poor Miss Molly–you have suffered terribly, and with your aunt now gone, it is…" she began, but a voice from the corridor caused her to startle.

"Lucy? Have you finished making the beds?" Mrs. Mallory called out.

Molly looked imploringly up at Lucy, who now had tears in her eyes.

"Please?" she whispered, thrusting the coins into Lucy's hand, and the maid nodded, pointing Molly to the wardrobe, and urging her to hide.

"Yes, Mrs. Mallory, I am just coming," she called back, and winking at Molly, she hurried out of the room.

Molly hid herself in the wardrobe. She could see through the keyhole, and she watched as Mrs. Mallory entered the room and inspected the bed. She was tutting to herself, muttering something about the corners of the bed not being exactly in their alignment. Molly despised her and seeing her in that moment only spurred her on in her intentions to leave Wisgate Grange and all its misery behind.

"Foolish girl," Mrs. Mallory exclaimed, picking up the discarded linen Lucy had forgotten to take in her haste and leaving the room.

Molly waited a moment before letting herself out of the wardrobe and returning to the nursery. Tobias had been playing with his toys, all of which were scattered carelessly across the floor. Molly readied her things, and she pulled out the box of treasures from beneath the bed, opening it to remind herself of why she was doing what she was doing. Like Rosedene, itself, the box was a tangible reminder of her aunt, and she felt close to her in that moment, happy to at last be escaping the misery of her lot.

"I will be a performer, Aunt Sally. I know I will," she said, closing the box and replacing it beneath the bed, her mind made up as to what was to come.

***

It all seemed so simple in Molly's mind—even if she knew it would not be. She had prepared a small bag with clothes, food, and the money she had found at Rosedene. This she hid in the shrubbery, and Molly would collect it as she made her way to the performance that evening. Lucy had bought the tickets and promised to leave the side door from the servant's corridor open—it led directly into the garden, and Molly could slip through the hedge and make her way into the village. After the performance, she would collect her bag from its second hiding place—the garden of Rosedene—and then make her way to the caravans of the performers, all of which were pulled up on the village green. There was to be only one performance and, just like last time, the troupe would leave Wisgate in the middle of the night, making for their next destination.

"And then I will be a performer," Molly told herself, as she sat watching the clock in the nursery, waiting for the appointed hour to leave.

But it was that point which caused her the most trepidation. Would the dancehall troupe accept her? Would they allow her to remain? Or would they simply return her to her father so that she might suffer the humiliation of his punishment, which was bound to be severe? It was a risk she will take, even as she knew the possibility of its consequences, and as dusk fell outside, she put on her shawl, took up a candle, and prepared to creep downstairs.

"Where are you going?" Tobias asked, catching her as she left the nursery.

He should already have been in bed, but he had a nasty habit of sneaking around the house at night, and now he stood looking at her with a horrible expression on his face.

"I am going to get a glass of milk," she said.

"You never drink milk in the evening," he retorted.

Molly's hands were trembling. She knew how easily he could betray her. He would follow her downstairs, he would shout and scream and their father and Mrs. Mallory would come running.

"And I was going to fetch a blanket from the linen cupboard," she said, a plan suddenly forming in her mind.

The linen cupboard lay up a flight of steps in the lower part of the attic. It was big enough to step inside, the walls lined with shelves containing piles of neatly folded bedding and blankets. They always left the key in the lock so that any member of the household might help themselves to bedding, should the need arise.

"I want one," Tobias said, for whatever Molly wished for, Tobias would take.

"Then come and choose one, I shall reach it down for you," Molly said, and Tobias nodded, following her up the steps to the attic.

She unlocked the door, opening it and pointing to the blankets on one of the lower shelves.

"I want the blue one," Tobias said, and Molly smiled.

"Then choose it," she said, and with a deft movement, she pushed Tobias into the linen cupboard, closing the door behind him and turning the key in the lock.

He screamed and began banging on the cupboard door, but Molly knew no one would hear him—not until the morning, at least, when the maids would come to make the beds with fresh sheets. She smiled to herself, making her way back down to the landing below and closing the door to the attic. Tobias' screams of anger were now completely muffled, and there was no sound of them at all as Molly crept downstairs and across the hallway. A chink of light came from beneath the door of her father's study. He would read and retire late, Mrs. Mallory having taken him a glass of brandy before she made her way to her private sitting room where she would spend the evening writing letters to her sisters. Molly knew the routine of the house precisely and had used that knowledge to concoct her plan. Now, she hurried along the servant's corridor, undisturbed, for all the servants had gone to the performance, and let herself out into the garden by the side door.

"*Freedom,*" she said to herself, slipping through the shadows and finding her bag as she had left it in the shrubbery.

It was now only a simple matter of slipping through the hedge and along the lane, and Molly made her way to Rosedene, where the outline of the house was visible across the garden in the moonlight. There was a sweet scent of roses in the air, and having hidden her bag, Molly took out a volume of verse her aunt had once given her. It had been a gift for her birthday, and she stowed several red petals inside it, intent on taking a little piece of her inheritance with her, wherever fortune might lead her.

"Goodbye Aunt Sally–I am going on an adventure," Molly said, and she slipped out of the garden and hurried towards the village, excited at the prospect of seeing the performance and reliving the memories she had so often dreamed of.

Chapter 8
The Marvellous Marvolo

"Roll up, roll up, roll up. Algernon Trott's spectacular travelling dancehall has come to Wisgate once again. Daring acts, remarkable magic, danger, and mystery. We have it all," the master of ceremonies declared, somersaulting onto the stage and leaping high up into the air.

Molly had arrived just in time and was sitting close to the back of the church hall, her heart racing with excitement at the prospect of what she was about to see. Every ticket had been sold, and there was an air of eager expectation amongst the audience as they waited for the performance to begin.

"Ah, Molly—you made it," the curate, Mr. Crockford said, and Molly turned to find him edging into the seat next to her, followed by his wife, who beamed at Molly as now the first of the performers came onto the stage in a flourish of cartwheels and acrobatic leaps.

"Yes… my father was… very generous in allowing me to come alone," Molly replied.

"Your dear aunt would have loved to see the performance. It is such a tragedy she is not here to do so," the curate replied, shaking his head.

"Pay attention, Mr. Crockford–the performance is starting," his wife said, and to Molly's relief, their attentions were now turned to the stage.

The acrobats concluded their performance to shouts of acclamation and applause, followed by the magician who produced reams of handkerchiefs from his assistant's ears, much to the glee of the children sitting in the front row who squealed with delight. The arrival of a rabbit from a large top hat only adding to their excitement. But it was Mr. Marvolo whom Molly had most been looking forward to seeing, and his appearance brought a hush over the audience as he stepped slowly into the middle of the stage.

"Good evening, my friends. What you are about to witness is to be my most dangerous and life-threatening feat to date. No one has yet seen this marvel, the marvel for which Mr. Marvolo will surely now be known," he exclaimed, as a whispered exclamation went around the audience.

"What do you suppose he will do?" Mr. Crockford exclaimed, pulling out his handkerchief and mopping his brow.

"Something remarkable," Molly replied, watching as Mr. Marvolo now summoned his assistant, who brought him two metal rods, each with a burning head attached, handing them to the performer with a flourish.

"Not one, but two torches," Mr. Marvolo said, and now an unseen musician began to play a deep sounding instrument, the beat of which rose with the tension now building on the stage.

Mr. Marvolo arched his back and with a flourish, he appeared to consume the entire torch, before drawing it back out of his mouth and breathing fire six feet into the air. The audience gasped, and now he brought the second torch across the length of his arm. He was wearing a waistcoat, the skin of his arms bare, and now the flames took hold of him, so that the performer himself was on fire.

"Good heavens, he shall burn to death," Mr. Crockford exclaimed, but Molly shook her head, watching in fascination as Mr. Marvolo rolled across the floor, leaping up in a burst of flame, which was suddenly extinguished.

"The flames do not consume," he cried out, and now he plunged the first of his torches back into his mouth, breathing out the flames as the audience gasped and applauded.

Molly was on her feet, cheering in amazement at the spectacle they had just witnessed. She thought of her aunt, and how astounded she would have been to see it.

"He surely lives up to his name," the curate's wife said, as Mr. Marvolo now took a deep bow and lauded his assistant who curtsied, before the two of them hurried off the stage.

"I have seen nothing like it before," Molly said, still unable to believe what she had seen.

The performances continued, and if Molly had for so long dreamed of being amongst them, the sight of the spectacle only further confirmed her desire. When at last the evening ended, the troupe returned as one to the stage, taking a bow as Algernon Trott himself stepped forward. He was a small man, dressed in an enormous top hat almost the size of him, and he wore a brightly coloured bow tie, red breeches, and a white coat, his hands raised in adulation at the applause.

"Thank you, thank you, a thousand times thank you," he exclaimed, before commending the performers to the audience, who continued to clap and cheer.

"You will not sleep tonight, Molly. You will be far too excited," Mr. Crockford said, as he and his wife walked with Molly out of the church hall a short while later.

"I do not think I will," Molly replied, though for very different reasons than the curate believed.

She bid them goodnight and hurried back to Rosedene to collect her bag from its hiding place amongst the rhododendrons. It felt strange to be saying goodbye, and she wondered when she would see her inheritance again. But she had no regrets in leaving Wisgate, no fear of the upset she would cause. Her mind was made up, and she took a deep breath, taking up her bag and setting her sights on the future.

***

The village green was dark, the moon casting silvery shadows through the three great oaks trees which stood in a triangle there and which gave the village inn its name. The houses surrounding the green were dark, and the church bell had just tolled the one O'clock hour. Molly stood in the shadows by the lychgate which led into the churchyard, peering at the silhouettes of the caravans and wondering what to do next. This was the part of the plan she had given little consideration to, and now she had run away. The question of what to do next loomed large.

"I need to hide somewhere," she told herself, for she had at least decided to accompany the dancehall troupe on the next leg of their journey, hoping that they would take pity on her when her inevitable discovery was made.

The caravans—each richly decorated like those of the gypsies—were arranged in a semi-circle, the smouldering remains of a fire sitting in the centre, and Molly crept forward, hoping to find one which was unoccupied. Snoring came from the caravan nearest the church, and Molly wondered if this was Mr. Marvolo, dreaming of his next feat of daring. The acrobats occupied the second caravan—Molly could see them asleep in a row of bunk beds through one of the small windows. But the next caravan appeared to contain the animals—the sounds of clucking, chirruping, and rustling emanating from beneath the ornately decorated door.

She paused, taking a deep breath, and knowing this could be her only chance. She tried the door, which, to her surprise, was unlocked. It opened into a space lined with cages, inside of which sat or perched the animals. Several of them peered at her curiously, but they were so tame that they made no sudden movement or noise, and Molly crept inside, closing the door behind her, and peering through the darkness for a place to hide. A shaft of moonlight was coming through one of the small windows in the side of the caravan and Molly could see an enormous pile of straw against the far wall. She buried herself beneath it, completely covered and feeling remarkably warm and snug.

"I have made it, I have run away," she said to herself, amazed by her own accomplishment.

It made her smile to think of Mrs. Mallory discovering Tobias locked in the linen cupboard the following morning, and of the look on her father's face when her escape was discovered. He would be livid with anger—not because he desired her return, but because she had disobeyed him. Tiredness now crept over her, and she yawned, burying herself further down into the straw and falling asleep.

***

Molly awoke with a jolt, and she sat up, forgetting for a moment where she was. Sunlight was streaming through the windows of the caravan, and the animals in their cages were scratching, scraping, tweeting, and clucking. The caravan had —its motion jolting Molly awake. She ached all over, and stretched out her arms, rising wobbly to her feet as the caravan rocked back and forth. It made her smile to think she had gotten away with hiding in the straw, though it seemed no one had yet entered the caravan that day, and cautiously, she peered out of the window to get a sense of their direction.

They were passing the outlying houses of the village, and Molly knew this was the road which would take them north, past her cousin's house at Wisgate Manor and on over farmland towards the town of Barlowe where the next performance was to be held. She could see several of the acrobats walking next to the caravans and occasionally they would perform a somersault, or cartwheel forward, clapping their hands together in delight at a successful trick. It was mesmerizing to watch.

"Oh, bravo, Reggie, you can do that with your eyes closed," she heard one performer say, and the one called Reggie took a bow and performed a further set of cartwheels, much to the delight of the others.

Molly now looked more carefully at her surroundings. There must have been twenty or so cages lining the walls of the cramped caravan, each containing an exotic looking animal, none of which would have seemed out of place in one of her aunt's books about faraway places. There was a parrot whose cage hung from the ceiling by the door, and who cocked its head to one side as Molly approached.

"Cracker?" it said, and Molly smiled.

"I do not have a cracker," she replied, and the parrot made a high-pitched laughing sound.

"No cracker, no talkie," it said, and turned its back on her.

Molly could not help but laugh, even as the parrot glanced over its shoulder in the vain hope she might still produce what it desired. The other cages contained smaller birds, some with remarkable plumage, others with elegant crests, or patterned wings, and Molly marvelled to see them, fascinated to think of the places they had come from—the same places, perhaps, where aunt had visited and explored.

"You are all quite remarkable," she said, peering down into the cages and shaking her head.

But as she did so, a noise outside caused her to startle and she could hear footsteps clambering up to the door. There was no time to think, and she dived into the straw, covering herself over just as the door opened and someone entered the caravan.

"I wish he had slowed up. I called to him to slow the horse. How can we climb up here when he is charging along with no thought for the poor horse's feet?" a woman's voice came from above.

Molly held her breath, praying they would not take up a bundle of straw—all which lay between her and discovery.

"You know what old Biggins is like. A law unto himself, one law for Biggins, another for us. Now then Pollyanna, what are you saying?" a man's voice asked, and Molly heard the parrot shift on its perch, flapping its wings before replying.

"No cracker, no cracker," it said, and the man laughed.

"I have not offered you a cracker yet, Pollyanna. But if you shall take that attitude, then I shall not do so, either," he said, and the woman laughed.

"Oh, Bill, we both know you will—and she does, too," she said, and the man laughed.

"You are right. There is no point in denying it. She shall have her cracker," he said, and now there came the sound of the cage being opened and the parrot devouring the cracker which Bill had given her.

"Does the straw need changing?" the woman asked, and Molly's heart skipped a beat.

"No, I changed it yesterday. Wait until we arrive at Barlowe. I want to walk in the sunshine. It is a beautiful day," he replied, and having fed the animals, the man and woman climbed down from the caravan, calling for the driver to slow up.

Molly breathed a sigh of relief, and climbed out from the straw, as Pollyanna now looked at her and squawked.

"Got my cracker," she said, and Molly smiled.

"And I think I shall have mine, too," she said, opening her bag and taking out two pieces of bread and dripping which she had sandwiched together before leaving Wisgate Grange the day before.

Her absence would now have been discovered. A search would be underway, the entire village roused. Her father would claim abduction, or a terrible accident, for he would never admit that it was he who had driven her away. Tobias would tell his story, and Mrs. Mallory would reward him with a large piece of cake and the sympathy of her attentions. It made Molly smile to think about it, even as she knew the danger she now faced. At some point soon she would have to reveal herself, and in doing so they would either send her back to her father–though if she were she would run away again–or be allowed to continue with the troupe. She had weighed up the possibilities in her mind and was determined to do all she could to persuade the performers to allow her to remain.

"They are certain to accept me when they discover my talent for performing," she told herself.

The caravans wended their way along country lanes for much of the day, and no further disturbances came, so that Molly could sit on the floor next to Pollyanna's cage, talking to the parrot as though she were making a new friend.

"Cracker?" the parrot would say, and Molly had found that a crust of bread was an adequate substitute for the request, one which she was happy to oblige the creature with, in return for its company.

"You are a clever parrot," she remarked, after Pollyanna had counted to three forwards and then backwards.

"Clever, clever, clever!" Pollyanna repeated, and Molly laughed.

"I wish I had known you years ago—we could have been friends," she replied, imagining a parrot perched in her aunt's parlour at Rosedene.

Her aunt would have found the entire adventure a delight, and whilst Molly was feeling trepidation of what lay ahead, she was certain that her aunt's courageous spirit would carry her through.

"You are just as I was when I was your age," her aunt had so often told her, and the memory of these words gave Molly the courage she needed.

It was dusk when the caravans came to a final halt, and Molly hid herself beneath the straw, imagining that Bill and his companion would soon return to see to the animals. She knew she would be discovered eventually but hoped to put as much distance between herself and Wisgate as possible before her presence was known. A short while after they had halted, Molly heard footsteps outside the door, and the flash of lantern now filled the caravan, the voice of Bill calling out a cheery greeting to Pollyanna.

"Now then, my dear, what naughtiness have you been getting up to today, and... oh, what is all this then?" Bill said, and Molly now heard another set of footsteps enter the caravan.

"Crumbs, all over the floor," a woman's voice–the same as had accompanied Bill earlier–said.

Molly held her breath. She had not thought about the crumbs from the crusts of bread, dropped by Pollyanna as she hungrily devoured the food they had shared earlier on.

"I gave her no bread," Bill said.

"Well, do not look at me–I have been nowhere near the caravan today. Not since we checked on the animals this morning. One other must have been in here feeding her. You know how Marvolo likes to make a fuss of them," the woman said.

"But the door was locked," Bill replied, and now Molly heard his footsteps approaching the pile of straw.

Her whole body was trembling. She knew that discovery was inevitable, and without waiting for Bill's hand to search her out, she burst out from the pile, causing the woman to scream at the top of her voice. Bill, too, fell back, his eyes wide with astonishment.

Chapter 9
A Mixed Welcome

"I am so sorry," Molly cried out, fearing for what they would do to her.

She imagined rough hands hauling her out of the caravan, angry voices raised against her–this had all been a terrible mistake.

"My word, a stowaway," Bill said, scrambling to his feet.

Molly cowered back, shaking her head, hardly able to speak for fear of what would happen.

"I… I am sorry, I was just–" she began, as tears welled up in her eyes.

"Hiding in the straw–she must have been here this morning? Was it you who fed Pollyanna?" the woman asked, stepping forward, her initial shock turned to curiosity.

"I did. She was asking for a cracker, but I only had a crust of bread," Molly replied, glancing at Pollyanna, who was squawking on her perch.

"How did you get in here? Have you been here since we left Wisgate?" Bill asked, and Molly nodded.

"I slipped in during the night. I am sorry, I had nowhere else to go. I was not thinking, I just… ran away," she said, and the woman shook her head in disbelief.

"But you are only a child. What could you be running away from? And why with us?" she asked.

Molly had pictured this moment dozens of times. She had practised her speech–how she would tell the performers of her desire to join them, and how they would ask her to juggle or sing. It had all seemed so easy in her mind, but now, faced with Bill and his companion, Molly could barely find the words to explain herself, let alone the courage to perform. She had packed the juggling balls her aunt had given her, but in that moment, they seemed of little use as she stammered her reply.

"Please, I mean no harm. But I had to leave. I saw your performance when I was very young. My aunt took me to it, but she died… only recently. I had to run away, I could not stay, my father–oh," she began, the emotion overwhelming her, and she sank to her knees and sobbed.

"The poor child. She has suffered some terrible ordeal," the woman said, and she came to kneel next to Molly and put her arms around her.

"We should tell Algernon–he will not like it," Bill said, but the woman looked up at him and shook her head.

"Algernon likes nothing – but, look at her, the poor child. She is desperate. We must help her. Where are you going?" she asked, cupping Molly's face in her hands and looking at her with a puzzled expression.

"I… I want to go with you," Molly replied, and the woman stared at her in amazement.

"With the dancehall troupe?" Molly nodded in return.

Molly liked this woman with long, ginger hair which hung in ringlets over her shoulders, and a large, hooped gold earring in her ear. She was wearing a simple, flower-patterned dress, and her rosy cheeks and smiling face made Molly feel as though she was someone who could be trusted. She recognised her as a magician, and Bill, too–he was the man who had made a rabbit appear out of a hat at the performance the night before, a tall man with dark hair and a handsome face, dressed in a green waistcoat, shirt, and breeches.

"She cannot stay hidden in the straw all night. Bring her outside, we can see what the others say," he said, and the woman offered Molly her hand.

"What is your name? Mine is Cecilia, but everyone calls me Celi," she said, and Molly smiled.

"I am Molly," she replied, grateful for the woman's kindness.

"And this is Bill," Celi said, pointing to Bill, who nodded.

"I heard your name this morning and I think your animals are wonderful–Pollyanna, especially," Molly said, glancing at the parrot, who cawed in response.

"I am surprised they did not make a terrible racket at your being here. They must like you," Bill replied, as now they stepped out of the caravan into the early evening sunlight.

They were halted in a field. Molly could see the spire of Barlowe church in the distance, and she knew they had come some fifteen miles from Wisgate. A stream ran along the edge of the field, which must have belonged to one of the local farmers, for some cattle were grazing in the far corner, paying no attention to the caravans which were arranged in the same semi-circle as they had been on the village green at Wisgate.

"Bill, Celi, fetch some water from the stream. The others will get the fire going," a voice came from one of the other caravans.

"Algernon, I think you had better see this," Celi called back, and a moment later, the face of Algernon Trott appeared from one caravan.

He was no longer wearing his top hat and tails, and without them, he looked rather plain, his face covered in dots of shaving cream, as he held a towel to his face, an open razor blade in his hand.

"What is it, Celi? Can you not see I am–oh," he said, staring at Molly, as now others emerged from their caravans to see what was going on.

Molly shrank back as curious eyes fell on her. There were around a dozen performers, all of whom she recognised from the evening before, amongst them, Mr. Marvolo, who now stepped forward and tutted.

"A stowaway?" he asked.

"She was hiding in the straw in the animals' caravan. She says she has run away–she is in a terrible state," Celi said, as Algernon Trott now hurried down the steps of his caravan, tossing aside the razor blade and towel as he did so.

"We cannot have this. Where did she come from? We must send her home. What has she told you?" he demanded.

"Only that she has run away. It is something to do with her aunt and her father. Do not be angry with her, Algernon. She is only a child," Celi said.

"But what are we supposed to do with a child?" Mr. Marvolo asked.

Despite some of them being overly tall or overly short, they all seemed remarkably normal without their costumes, dressed in clothes such as any ordinary person in Wisgate would wear. Molly had expected magic, mystery, but this... it all seemed remarkably mundane.

"Send her back," Algernon said, but Molly shook her head, tears now welling up in her eyes as suddenly she found her voice.

"Please, no, do not send me back, I beg you," she cried, and they stared at her in amazement.

"She speaks," Mr. Marvolo said, as now the others gathered around.

There was the tall man Molly remembered from the parade when she was a young child, and the short man who wore the exaggerated top hat and tails, dressed now in an open shirt and short breeches. The woman with long hair was there, and next to her, the man who tamed the elephant, which was standing chewing hay by the brook, tethered to a tree.

"Please, I cannot go back–it would be too awful. My father has been cruel to me, and he will be crueller still if you send me back. I want to be a performer. It is all I have ever dreamed of, all my aunt ever dreamed of," Molly said, and Mr. Marvolo laughed.

"You? A performer? What a notion. But you are only a child. What skills do you have?" he demanded.

"You were a child once, Marvolo," his assistant, a blonde-haired woman in a blue silk dress named Talia, remarked.

"Well, yes, but I did not think I could be a performer then," he replied.

Molly was shaking, but in her hand, she held the bag containing the juggling balls given to her by her aunt. This was it. This was her moment, the moment she had so long been preparing for. The memory of all those hours spent in the garden at Rosedene or in the parlour flashed across her mind with her aunt's encouraging words.

"You can do it, Molly–follow your dreams," she heard her aunt saying, and Molly took a deep breath and opened the bag.

"Juggling balls?" Celi said, a note of surprise in her voice.

"They belonged to my Aunt Sally. She gave me them when I was seven years old, and I have practised with them ever since," Molly said.

"What a thing, indeed," Algernon said, and the others whispered between themselves, watching as Molly took the three balls in hand and closed her eyes.

"But you cannot juggle with eyes closed," Mr. Marvolo said.

But Moly paid no heed, and she threw the first ball into the air, followed by the second, and then the third. It was just as she had practised. The balls passing from one hand to the next, circling up in an arc and back down to begin the process again. She opened her eyes, a smile breaking over her face at the sight of the performers all watching in amazement.

"You see," Celi said, and Algernon clapped his hands together in delight.

"Well, that is a thing indeed," Mr. Marvolo said, and Molly now threw the balls up higher, jigging from foot to foot as the others clapped in delight.

"And she dances, too," Algernon exclaimed.

Molly now caught all three balls and gave a bow. She had never performed for anyone before–only her aunt–but the feeling she felt at their adulation was quite remarkable. She smiled as Celi put her arm around her and congratulated her.

"I have never seen someone so young perform in such a way before. You were marvellous, Molly," she said.

"I have been practicing for many years, but I know I could do better. I only want to perform. It is all I have ever dreamed of, ever since my aunt took me to see your performance all those years ago," she said.

"And you have held onto that dream ever since?" Algernon asked.

"It is the only thing that has made me happy," Molly admitted, feeling the tears rising in her eyes once more.

"What a remarkable story," Mr. Marvolo said, the scepticism in his voice now gone.

"And you say you want to stay with us? That you ran away to join us? But what of your parents? Will no one be looking for you?" Algernon asked.

"They will look, but I do not want to be found. My Aunt Sally is dead, and she was my only friend in all the world. She–" Molly began, but the tall man was looking at her intently and he interrupted her now, stepping forward to get a better look at her.

"What was your aunt's name? Sally what?" he asked.

"Fletcher, but Walden before she was married—she was a remarkable woman," Molly said, and the man smiled.

"I think I remember her. I remember her performing, but there was a scandal—she was of a good name, I did not think it appropriate," he said, and Molly nodded.

"She wanted to be a performer, but she could not be one. My family thought it foolish. She never could follow her dream," Molly said, shaking her head sadly.

"Then her niece shall," Algernon said, and Molly looked up at him in wide-eyed amazement.

"Do you mean it? I can come with you?" she exclaimed, and he nodded.

"You will have to work your way, and you shall have to practise and appear on stage. It is not an easy life, you know. But… we are all of us outcasts, Molly. We all have a story to tell—we do not all fit in to what convention tells us is right. Perhaps we are all running away from something. There is a place for you here. I have a feeling about it," he said, and Molly beamed at him.

"Oh, thank you, a thousand times, thank you," she said, hardly daring to believe it was true.

She had never found a place—not truly. Rosedene had been a refuge, but someone had always forced her to return from it, to step back into the world and suffer the grim reality which was her true life. But now, perhaps things could be different. Perhaps she had found what she had always longed for.

"A new performer in the troupe, we have not added to our number in many years," Mr. Marvolo said, shaking his head.

But he smiled at Molly, as did the others, and the suspicious glances now turned to a warm welcome. They showed her to one caravan, where a bunk bed–the other occupied by Celi–was built into an alcove in the wall.

"You can sleep in here with me. It will be pleasant company," Celi said, and Molly looked around her at the caravan, which felt snug and cosy, its walls ornately decorated and many trinkets piled here and there.

"Is that the magician's top hat?" she asked, pointing to an oversized hat which sat on a chair in the corner.

"It is, but he will not tell you the secret of it," Celi said, smiling at Molly, who gazed at the hat in wide-eyed amazement.

"I am so happy to be staying with you all. It has been my dream for longer than I can remember. I thought you would send me back," she said, turning to Celi, who smiled and shook her head.

"I think you will fit in well here. We are all a little lost. I ran away myself–I lived with my stepmother, and she was ever so cruel to me. But come now, we must have something to eat and then see to the animals. You can help me if you like," she said.

Molly was eager to help in any way she could, and she followed Celi out of the caravan–which felt like a new home– and over to where a fire had a cooking pot suspended on a tripod. Mr. Marvolo was tending to the flames, blowing them gently so raise the flame, as his assistant added kindling to help it burn.

"I do not just eat it," he said, and Molly laughed.

"I think you are remarkable—all of you," she said, and Mr. Marvolo looked up and laughed.

"Tricks, illusions, conjuring—that is all. It is the spectacle that matters. Take fire eating. It is an art, of course, but I do not really burn myself—I come to no harm," he said, even as his assistant tutted and shook her head.

"Rarely, at least," she said, and Mr. Marvolo smiled.

"It is the risk one takes—I would not wish to be a bookkeeper, or a lawyer, or a schoolmaster, and so—" he began, but Celi interrupted him.

"And so you became a fire eater instead," she said, shaking her head and laughing.

"Precisely," he replied, and with a final blow, he summoned the flames into life.

Molly was now invited to sit, and the rest of the performers came to join them, some of them bringing vegetables for the pot, and others wood for the fire. A delightful smell now wafted over the camp, and it was not long before the meal was ready, and bowls and spoons were handed around, along with slices of bread to eat to eat with the stew.

"And what other skills do you have, Molly? What else are we to discover about you? Do you sing or dance? Can you pull a rabbit out of a hat?" Algernon Trott asked, when Molly had finished eating.

"Let her settle first, Algernon—perhaps there is something she would like to learn. She has a natural talent for performing. It only needs to be encouraged," Celi said, but Molly was determined to prove her worth.

"I can sing a little. My aunt played the piano, you see. And I love to dance. I have practised a few magic tricks, but they often go wrong–I did once make a coin appear from my aunt's ear and she could not tell how I had done it," Molly said, thinking fondly of her aunt and wondering what she would say if she could see her now.

"You and your aunt were very close, it seems," Algernon said, and Molly nodded.

"I miss her terribly," she said, for though in that moment she felt happier than she had done in a very long time, the tragic loss of her aunt still weighed heavily on her–she would never forget her, and she knew her spirit would forever be with her.

"It is the price we pay for love–loss," Mr. Marvolo said, and Molly looked up at him, his eyes betraying a pain she knew, too.

"But better to have loved and lost than never to have known love at all," Algernon said.

"But if only the world were not so cruel," Mr. Marvolo said, and Molly wondered what the source of his pain might be.

"Enough of this talk. We do not want to upset Molly before she has even settled herself amongst us," Celi said, rising to her feet.

"Yes, we should see to the animals–it will be dark soon," Bill said, and he beckoned Molly to follow them.

They found Pollyanna asleep on her perch and the rest of the small animals curled up in their straw or munching on the feed which Celi and Bill had brought to them earlier that evening. Molly remained fascinated by the array of colours and plumage on display. She wanted to know all their names, where they came from, what they did.

"You will learn about them soon enough—we take great pride in them," Celi said, holding out a cracker to Pollyanna, who squawked and cawed in appreciation.

"How did she learn to talk?" Molly asked, looking at the parrot in fascination.

"They have to be taught from when they are very young," Bill said, holding out his arm so that Pollyanna could jump from her perch.

"Very young—old Bill," she said, and Bill laughed.

"She is really only repeating things she hears, but a part of me wonders whether she knows a lot more than we think," he said, stroking the parrot's feathers as she opened her wings and clacked her beak.

"Another cracker, Pollyanna?" Molly asked, holding up a cracker to the bird, who darted her beak forward and snatched the cracker from Molly's hand.

"Rude bird," Bill said, chastising Pollyanna, who laughed.

"She is just excited to meet a new friend. Come now, we should put fresh straw in the cages, otherwise it is just another job to do tomorrow morning," Celi said.

With Molly's help, they soon had the straw changed and they bedded all the animals down for the night. It was almost dark now, and only a few of the performers remained around the campfire. They would rise early the next day to prepare for the show in Barlowe that evening, and Molly—feeling exhausted after her night in the straw—followed Celi to the caravan where she was pleased to climb beneath sheets and wrap herself up in the alcove bunk to sleep.

"You have all been so kind to me," she said, as Celi climbed up into the bunk above.

"I am sure you will be happy with us—but you must say if you are not. We travel for many hundreds of miles in the season. It is not always easy, and it is better to realise now, rather than later, if this life is not for you," she replied.

But Molly's mind was firmly made up. This was the life she had imagined, the one she had dreamed of, and the one her aunt had desired, too. She would live it for them both, and as she fell asleep that night, Molly was certain her aunt was smiling down on her.

Chapter 10
Life on the Road

Molly was worried about the performance in Barlowe. She imagined her father or Mrs. Mallory bursting into the church hall where the show was taking place and demanding her return. She did not perform that night, watching from the side as Mr. Marvolo ate fire and Celi and Bill displayed their exotic animals. But no such thing occurred—no one asked about the girl gazing up in awe at the stage or wondered as to her parents. It seemed they had not connected her absence to the dancehall troupe, and if her father and Mrs. Mallory were looking for her, they were not looking for her in Barlowe.

After the evening's performance, life with the dancehall troupe settled down into a predictable regularity. They would travel from town to town, following a route which Celi told Molly they had followed for years, ever since Algernon had inherited the troupe from his father. They passed through large towns, small villages, and remote hamlets, bringing their performance to delighted crowds, who marvelled at their acts and showered them with adulation.

Little by little, Molly could take part further in the performances, and at first, she joined Celi and Bill on stage to display the animals. She was terribly nervous the first time she held Pollyanna out in front of the audience, but she need not have feared, for the parrot was happy to preen her feathers and make a show of herself. Molly talked to her, and the audience laughed as Pollyanna seemed to join in the conversation, making light of a rotund gentleman sitting in the front row.

"Too many crackers," she said, nodding her head towards him.

In this way, Molly grew in confidence, so much so that it was not long before Algernon and the others decided it was time for her to perform her own act. They had just arrived in Bath and were to perform at the assembly rooms there–a larger venue than they were used to, and with the expectation of drawing quite a crowd.

"You want me to juggle on stage?" Molly asked when Algernon suggested it.

"That is your act, Molly, and you are very good at it. Celi and Bill can manage Pollyanna and the other animals. But it is juggling and dancing I want you to display," he said, and Molly's eyes grew wide with delight.

As nervous as she felt, this was what she had been waiting for–the chance to perform in front of others and show her skills off to a real audience. She smiled at Algernon and nodded, imagining herself on stage and hearing the cheers and cries of adulation from all around.

"You should practise–juggling, dancing, perhaps you could sing a song," Algernon said, and smiling at Molly, he ambled off across the field where they had made camp the previous evening.

"How exciting for you," Celi said, when Molly told her what was to happen.

"This is what I have been waiting for—I just hope I can do it," she replied, feeling suddenly more nervous at the prospect of what was to come.

She had practised long and hard. She could juggle blindfolded, and with four balls, too. But to do so in front of a real audience, to be the one on whom all eyes were turned… her heart was beating fast at the prospect, and now she returned to her and Celi's caravan to practise. She took out her aunt's juggling balls, closed her eyes, and threw the first one into the air. It fell to the ground with a thud, and she opened her eyes in horror, her hand still outstretched with an open palm.

"Why did I not catch it?" she exclaimed, and she scolded herself for not concentrating.

Now, she took a deep breath and threw a second ball up into the air, willing herself to catch it and knowing that everything depended on the coming night.

***

"Roll up, roll up, roll up—Algernon Trott's dancehall spectacular is about to begin. See the magic, experience the mystery, and be amazed by daring feats and remarkable sights right before your very eyes!" Algernon Trott was saying.

Molly was standing in the wings. The assembly rooms were like nothing she had ever seen before—a theatre with plush, red velvet curtains, and rows and rows of seats, all filled with fashionable ladies and gentlemen come to see the performance. The troupe was used to church halls, the back room of a tavern, or a farmer's barn–but this was something very different. Molly had not eaten her dinner, so nervous had she felt, and now she stood with Celi and Bill, knowing her time was soon to come.

"You will be all right, Molly–think how hard you have practised," Bill said, putting his arm around her.

"I have never seen a better juggler than you, Molly–not at such a young age. Just believe you can do it and you will," Celi said.

She was holding Pollyanna in her cage, and the parrot squawked as though she, too, were encouraging Molly in what was to come.

"I have done everything I can to prepare," Molly said, clutching the juggling balls in her hands.

She thought back to those afternoons at Rosedene, the stage built of packing cases and her aunt sitting with Clive, the puppet, on a large armchair in front, clapping and cheering her on. How she wished her aunt was there now to encourage her, and she brushed a tear from her eye as Algernon now announced her performance.

"A remarkable act for you now, ladies and gentlemen–a young lady who will juggle not one… not two… not three… but four juggling balls–blindfolded!" he said with a flourish, pausing as the audience oohed in response.

"Good luck, forget the audience, just enjoy yourself," Celi said, and Molly took a deep breath and ran out onto the stage as applause filled the air.

It was Algernon who tied the blindfold over her eyes. He did it with much theatrics, flourishing the red and white spotted handkerchief and draping it over her face, so that all was dark. Silence now descended over the audience, and Molly held out her hand, imagining that this was a practise like any other and that there were not several hundred people watching her from below. She threw the first ball up into the air, and, to her relief, it fell back into her palm, just as she tossed the next one, and the next, and the fourth into the air, the audience giving a delighted exclamation as Molly passed the juggling balls effortlessly between her hands. She could not help but smile, and now the music began, the cue for her to dance. She did so in an exaggerated manner, kicking her legs out and leaping into the air, all the while catching the balls which rose and fell in an arc, up and down, the rhythm of the music matching the rhythm of the juggling balls. Molly could not have felt happier in that moment, knowing she was fulfilling her dream and that of her aunt.

"Bravo, simply remarkable–the marvellous Molly," Algernon said, clapping as Molly's performance ended.

She caught the juggling balls and Algernon removed the blindfold so that she could look out at the audience. The assembly rooms were lit by gas lights, and though they had been turned down for the performance, their flicker still illuminated the rows of well-dressed men and women applauding riotously. Molly stepped forward and bowed, and as she did so, her eyes met those of a boy not much older than herself, sitting in the front row. He was dressed to match the man next to him, in black breeches and a light green frock coat, his collar was starched up around his neck, and he wore a yellow cravat, his blonde hair combed back and a look of the utmost admiration on his face.

"Thank you," Molly said, as she rose from her bow and looked out over the audience, but as she hurried off stage, she could not rid herself of the image of the boy watching her from the audience.

"You were wonderful, Molly–absolutely wonderful. Did you enjoy it?" Celi asked, throwing her arms around Molly and kissing her.

"I did–I loved it. I can hardly describe how I feel. It is like nothing I have experienced before," she said, filled with such elation that her heart felt fit to burst.

"Enjoy the moment–it is why we do what we do," Bill said, just as Mr. Marvolo came hurrying over to them.

"Have I missed my cue?" he demanded.

"Algernon is still extolling you," Celi replied, and Mr. Marvolo gave an exaggerated cry, bringing the back of his palm to his face and sighing.

"Marvellous, I need a moment to compose myself," he exclaimed, as his assistant, Talia, hurried up behind him.

"Come along, Marvolo, it's time," she said, pushing him towards the stage.

Molly giggled at the sight of Mr. Marvolo now throwing his hands up in the air as his assistant lit the burning torches and together, they made their way on stage.

"Will I always have this feeling?" she asked, and Celi nodded.

"Perhaps not with quite the same intensity. But yes, you shall always feel like this when you perform. It is why we do it. But you must rest now, Molly—there are dressing rooms through there," she said, pointing to a door in the wings.

Molly glimpsed Mr. Marvolo breathing fire, and she made her way from the stage and into the relative calm of the dressing room, where several of the acrobats were preparing for their performance.

"Algernon is pleased with you, Molly," one of them said, and they gave further congratulations as Molly sat down with a smile on her face.

She would gladly have performed again, eager to display her skills and hear the adulation of the audience. But as she sat thinking back to all that had happened that night, the face of the boy in the front row crossed her mind. It made her smile to think of the look on his face, as though he was in awe of her skills, just as she herself had been the first time she had seen the dancehall troupe perform.

***

"One of our best performances to date. I am proud of you all, but especially of Molly—she has shown her true worth," Algernon said, after the performers had gathered backstage after the last curtain call.

"Hear, hear," Mr. Marvolo said, and the others applauded.

Molly blushed—she enjoyed the adulation of the audience, but it felt embarrassing to be treated in such a way by her peers.

"We can expect great things from you, Molly, I am certain of it," Algernon said, just as a knock came at the door and one steward from the assembly rooms entered in his livery, beckoning to Algernon who straightened himself up and went to speak with him.

Molly watched as they whispered to one another, and Algernon nodded, glancing at Molly and smiling.

"Has something happened?" Molly asked, when Algernon had called her out of the room.

"It is nothing to worry about, Molly, but it seems your performance has caught the eye of the Duke of Thurlstone, who was in the audience this evening. He wants to meet you," Algernon said, and Molly stared at him in amazement.

She had only done that which she had practised, and to know her performance had been met with such appreciation was quite overwhelming.

"But… a duke?" she exclaimed, and Algernon nodded.

"And his son, too. They are waiting for you out here," he said, hurrying her along.

They went through a door and emerged into a brightly lit vestibule–the entrance to the assembly rooms. Fashionably dressed men and women were milling around, sharing refreshments and conversation. The liveried steward directed them towards an elderly man with silver hair and a kindly looking face, and to Molly's astonishment, he was accompanied by the boy from the audience, the one who had gazed at her with such rapture.

"Your Grace, may I present Mr. Algernon Trott and Miss Molly Walden," the steward said, bowing to the duke, who stepped forward and offered Molly his hand.

"A remarkable performance, Miss Walden. It captivated Michael," the duke said as Molly smiled at the boy, who nodded enthusiastically.

"I wish I could juggle like that–I wish I could perform, but... I can do nothing like that," he said, his face falling.

"It is just a matter of practise," Molly replied, smiling at the boy who shrugged and glanced up at his father who smiled.

"I wonder, Mr. Trott, if you might permit Miss Walden to come to our home at Rowlands Park tomorrow? It is only a few miles outside of Bath and I would send the carriage. I recently lost my dear wife, Michael's mother, and we are both somewhat... struggling... in the tragic aftermath. The distraction of this evening's performance has been a welcome tonic, and I know it would do Michael good to spend time with one such as Miss Walden. She might bring her juggling balls, too?" he said.

Algernon smiled, looking down at Molly, who nodded. She felt terribly sorry for Michael at hearing such sad news, and having lost her own mother and her aunt, she sympathised with how he was surely feeling. She wanted to help, and she reached out and took Michael's hand, smiling at him as she did so.

"It is all in the palms. You must open your palms and allow the balls to pass between them," she said, and he smiled.

"You make it sound terribly easy," he replied.

"I will show you tomorrow," she said, and at these words, his face lit up.

"You will come then?" he asked, glancing up at his father in delight, and Molly turned to Algernon, who nodded.

"We are to rest tomorrow before travelling on to our next destination. You can go–it will be good for you to spend time with one of your own age instead of us and that dratted parrot," he replied, smiling at her.

"Could you bring the parrot, too?" Michael asked, his eyes growing wide with delighted expectation.

"I will have to ask Celi and Bill, but I am sure I can. Her name is Pollyanna. You must have some crackers prepared for her," Molly said, and Michael clapped his hands together in delight.

The arrangements were made and the duke and his son bid them both goodnight.

"You have made that boy very happy, Molly," Algernon said, as they returned backstage to find the others.

"I know his sorrow. It is the same as mine–my aunt was like a mother to me, and to live without her is a terrible burden. But I know, too, that life can be better, that joy can come again–I found that here with all of you, and if I can bring a little joy to him, then I will gladly do so," she replied.

Molly was happy to help Michael and his father. She knew she could teach him to juggle just as her aunt had taught her, and the prospect of doing so filled her with expectant delight. She was the talk of the troupe that evening, and everyone congratulated her on her performance, but it was the thought of Michael's delight which pleased her the most. Proof that even amidst a terrible sorrow, they could still find joy.

Chapter 11
Rowlands Park

It was a grand carriage indeed, which arrived to bring Molly to Rowlands Park the next day. The duke had sent two liveried servants to accompany her, along with a hamper of delicious food and drink for the rest of the troupe, the message accompanying it thanking them all for bringing him and his son a little joy amidst the darkness of their current sorrow.

"I cannot imagine a kinder gentleman," Algernon said, as he and the others opened the hamper to reveal a side of ham, cheeses, preserves, a fruitcake, and bottles of beer and cider.

"Come along Pollyanna, the duke is waiting," Molly said, coaxing the parrot from Bill's arm.

"Be sure to watch her—you know what she can be like," Bill said, for he had taken some persuading to allow Pollyanna to accompany Molly to Rowlands Park that morning.

"I have plenty of crackers," Molly replied, and Pollyanna squawked.

"Crackers! Crackers!" she said, and the others laughed.

"We will see you when you get back, Molly," Celi said, helping her up into the carriage.

"I am sure I can teach him," Molly replied, and Celi smiled.

"I am sure you can, Molly. If anyone can, it is you," she said, closing the carriage door and waving Molly off.

The carriage drew away from the campsite, a strange sight next to the ancient gypsy caravans and the elephant, who stood ponderously chewing a mouthful of straw. Molly sat back with Pollyanna perched on her arm, smiling to herself at the strange direction her life had taken. If only her father could see her now.

***

It took an hour to reach the gates of Rowlands Park, and Molly stared out of the carriage window in awe at the sight of the house, which was bigger than any she had ever seen. Parkland stretched out on every side, tall oak trees growing at intervals, and a river running its course below the house, which was built in a classical style with a large colonnaded portico and wings on either side.

"Cracker?" Pollyanna asked, and Molly reached into her pocket and took out a cracker, feeding it to the parrot as she continued to marvel at the size of the house.

The carriage drew up a few moments later, and a footman hurried out to greet them, carrying with him a velvet covered step which he placed by the carriage door as Molly stepped out.

"Welcome to Rowlands Park, Miss Walden. His Grace is expecting you," he said, holding out his hand to show Molly the way.

She had brought the juggling balls in a bag, and the footman carried it for her, leading her up the steps and into a large entrance hall resplendent in black-and-white marble. Portraits hung on the walls, and a grand staircase, carpeted in the same red velvet shade, led up to a gallery above. Molly recognised the figures in the painting at the top of the stairs–the duke and Michael stood together in a classical garden, whilst in front of them sat a woman, exquisite, and who must surely have been Michael's mother.

"What a remarkable place," she said, and the footman bowed.

"I will fetch his Grace. He has been ever so excited to see you," the footman said, and he hurried off across the hallway, his shoes clacking on the marble floor.

Molly continued to gaze at her surroundings in awe. This was nothing like her cousin's home at Wisgate Manor, or her father's residence of Wisgate Grange. This was surely one of the grandest houses in all of England, and Molly could not help but be impressed.

"Miss Walden, you came, and you brought the parrot," a voice exclaimed, and Molly turned to find Michael running towards her, his face a picture of delight.

"Of course, I came–I promised to, did I not? Pollyanna has been eating crackers in the carriage for the past hour, but I am sure she would enjoy another," Molly said, as Michael now produced a cracker from his pocket and held it up tentatively to the parrot, who leaned forward and snatched it from his hand.

"Where are your manners, Pollyanna?" Molly exclaimed as Michael laughed.

"No manners, no manners," Pollyanna said, and Molly rolled her eyes.

At that moment, the duke himself appeared, and he welcomed Molly warmly to Rowlands Park.

"I have never seen such a house in all my life," she replied, staring up at the ceiling of the hallway, which was painted to appear as the sky at the breaking of the dawn.

"What of your origins, Molly? Where do you come from?" the duke asked, and Molly was glad to tell her tale, even as the duke shook his head and sighed.

"A father who mistreats his own daughter. What a terrible tragedy. Though how fortunate you were to have your dear aunt. I am truly sorry for your loss. Believe me when I say I understand it, as does Michael," the duke said, patting his son on the shoulder and bowing his head.

"I… I suppose one learns to live with such tragedy, even if it is hard to do so, and even if one never truly forgets," Molly replied.

"Time is a healer, that is very true, but the memory remains, and it change us. The tragedy changed us, but also by sharing in the life of that person. Your aunt made you so much of what you are today, Molly. Just as I see my darling Anne in Michael every day," he replied.

"May I take Molly to the drawing room, Father? We can practise our juggling there. I asked Mrs. Morrison to remove all the china," Michael said, and his father laughed.

"I am sure she will be in a state of the utmost panic at the thought of your juggling close to the Ming vases. But yes, the two of you must practise—I think it will make you happy to have someone to talk to, Michael," the duke said, and

Michael beckoned Molly to follow him through the hall and down a long corridor with doors going off on either side.

It felt strange to be amidst such grandeur, and yet to feel entirely at ease in being so. There was nothing grand or aloof about Michael and his father—they were simply two people whom Molly felt she could understand. After all, grief is the greatest of levellers, it comes to both rich and poor alike, and the tragic loss of death is just as heartfelt by prince and pauper both.

"In here," Michael said, opening a door which led into a room facing the gardens. They had pushed the furniture back, and the rug rolled back in front of the fire to create an open space in which they could practise. Molly set Pollyanna down on the mantelpiece and Michael took out a cracker, clearly delighting in the novelty of feeding the exotic bird.

"I brought the juggling balls with me," she said, taking them out of her bag, and Michael smiled, stepping back so that he could watch.

"I do envy you, Molly. I wish I could perform like you did last night," he said, and Molly laughed.

"Would it surprise you to know that was the first time I had ever performed on stage? With the juggling balls, I mean. I was terribly nervous, but I almost forgot the audience was there. I was concentrating so hard on keeping the balls in the air that nothing else seemed to matter," she replied, and Michael shook his head in amazement.

"But... you were magnificent," he exclaimed, and she blushed.

"I have practised long and hard, but you could do the same—if it is what you want," she replied, and he nodded, a wistful look coming over his face.

"My mother used to sing to me. She would sit at the piano over there and play as she sang," he said, pointing to a piano standing in the corner of the drawing room, covered over by an embroidered gold cloth.

"I know you must miss her terribly. I am the same in my feelings towards my aunt. I long for one more smile, one more touch of her hand, one more word," Molly said, and Michael nodded, his eyes filling with tears as he spoke.

"I just wish… I wish she was here. She used to say, "follow your dreams, Michael," and now I know what she meant by that," he said, and Molly nodded.

"Because you have seen me following mine?" she asked, and he smiled.

"I want to make her proud. I want to learn to do what you did last night," he said, pointing to the juggling balls which Molly had taken out of her bag.

She took one in her hand and threw it up in the air, catching it in her outstretched palm.

"One is easy—a child could catch one ball, and even two is not difficult," she said, taking up a second ball and tossing it up into the air, followed by the first, passing them between her hands in a circle.

"You make it look so easy. May I have a go?" he asked, and Molly tossed him first one and then the second.

He caught them and threw them both up in the air in quick succession, holding out the palms of his hands. But he was not quick enough, and they fell to the floor with a thud.

Pollyanna laughed, but Molly turned to her and tapped her sharply on the beak.

"How rude, Pollyanna–would you like it if laughed at you every time you dropped a cracker or slipped off your perch?" she asked, and the parrot fell silent.

"She is right to laugh–you said it would be easy," Michael said, but Molly only smiled and shook her head, reaching down to pick up the two balls before taking Michael by the hand.

"You must not be downhearted. Let me show you. First one and then next. Throw it up in the air and catch it, then pass it. Throw and catch, throw and catch, throw and catch. Keep repeating that you yourself over and over," she said, as Michael threw the first ball up in the air.

This time, he caught it, and as he did so, he tossed the second up in the air, catching that and repeating the cycle. A smile came over his face and he nodded as Molly clapped her hands together in delight.

"There now, you have mastered it–two balls, at least," she said, taking up a third as Michael continued to pass the first two between his hands.

"But you said yourself the third is far harder," he said, a tentative look coming over his face.

"And that is true–you will not master it the first time, or the second, or the third, but try it a hundred times and you will do so. Anything worth doing takes practise," she said, and Michael nodded, smiling at her as now she passed the remaining two balls between her hands.

"Do you want me to throw one into yours?" he asked, and she nodded.

"Throw it up high if you can, so that it joins the other in the air," she said, and Michael did so, the arcing up and falling into Molly's palm.

In an instant, she had given it lift, so that it joined the second ball in flight. The three now passed in a circle, hand to hand, and Molly smiled, looking up at the balls flying through the air.

"You make it look so easy, Molly," he said, shaking his head, his eyes wide with amazement as he watched her juggling the three balls together.

She had him pass her the fourth ball and soon she was throwing them up almost to the ceiling, always keeping three in the air and the fourth passed quickly from palm to palm. Michael stood watching in awe, and when at last she let the four balls fall, he clapped and jumped up and down in delight.

"You will do this one day–it is just like practising anything. You can do it if you really want to," she said, picking up the balls and giving a low bow.

"I will practise, I really will–you have inspired me. I feel… I feel so much happier than I did yesterday," he said, and it almost appeared there was a note of guilt in his voice, as if feeling happy was not right.

"I remember the first time I felt like that after my aunt had died. It was when Algernon and the others allowed me to go with them and join the troupe. It seemed as though I should not have felt happy, even though I did. I felt guilty, but I should not have done. Your dear mother would have wanted you to be happy, and if juggling makes you happy, then you must juggle," she said, looking at Michael, who nodded and sighed.

"You are right. I have been so terribly upset these past weeks. I thought I would never smile again, but... you have helped me do so, Molly," he said, and Molly reached out and took him by the hand.

"I am glad to have done so. You have helped me, too. I have met someone who understands how I feel, and that has made me feel much better," she said.

They stood for a moment with their hands clasped together, and it was Pollyanna who interrupted them, squawking, and opening her wings.

"Cracker?" she asked, and both Molly and Michael laughed.

"She will not allow us to forget her," Michael said, reaching into his pocket and pulling out a cracker, which he held up for Pollyanna to take.

She crunched it loudly, letting out a further squawk and clacking her beak.

"We must get you home, Pollyanna. Bill and Celi will be worried about you," Molly said, offering her arm to the bird.

"Must you go immediately? There are refreshments laid out in the dining room and I thought you might like to see the gardens. I would very much like it if you stayed a while longer," Michael said, and Molly smiled.

"I am sure they will not miss me if I remain a little longer," she replied, and Michael grinned at her.

"I am very pleased about that," he said, and he offered her his arm.

He led her–and Pollyanna–out of the drawing room and across the corridor into a dining room, the windows of which looked out over the gardens. The table was set with a magnificent array of cakes and savouries–far more than the mere "refreshments" which Michael had promised. It was a warm day, and Molly was glad of the jug of lemonade from which one footman poured them each a glass, as the maids brought yet more delicacies to the table.

"I have never seen so much food," Molly exclaimed, her eyes growing wide at the sight of the delicate cakes and sumptuous pastries now proffered.

"I thought you would be hungry after the performance last night. I want to hear all about it and your life with the dancehall troupe. It must be so exciting to travel the country and see so many new places, and the performances and the animals… oh, it is all so wonderful," Michael said, and he beckoned Molly to sit down, as the maids fussed around them with plates and napkins.

Molly found she had a great deal to say–her life was an adventure, one she revelled in everyday. Michael was right. There was so much she had seen and experienced since leaving Wisgate and it was fun to tell her new friend about the life she now lived.

"And Mr. Marvolo is my favourite. I can hardly believe it when he breathes in the fire and blows it out again like a dragon. It looks so dangerous, but he assures me it is not," Molly said, as Michael shook his head and smiled.

"I wish I could come with you. I am going to ask my father if we might come to see the next performance. You are only travelling a short distance, I believe–to a village east of Bath.

I am sure he will say yes. He enjoyed it as much as I did," Michael said, and Molly laughed.

"We will find you stowed away in the straw just like I," she said, but Michael's face fell, and he sighed.

"I wish you could find me like that. Some days I want to run away myself. Everything about Rowlands Park reminds me of my mother. I really miss her so much," he said, and Molly reached out and took him by the hand.

It was her own grief she could see etched on his face. He spoke of Rowlands Park as she might speak of Rosedene, where every sight and sound and smell reminded her of her aunt.

"I understand, but you have one thing I did not," she said, and he looked up at her in surprise.

"And what is that?" he asked.

"A father who loves you, and a father who needs you, too. Imagine how lonely he would be without you. Your place is here, and if you practise your skills, and have something other than your grief to dwell on… bit by bit, you will feel better. I know you will," she said, and he nodded.

"I was being foolish, I know. I am sorry. Your story is… terrible," he said, but she shook her head.

"It has had a happy ending. I think, at least," she replied, and he looked at her curiously.

"What do you mean by that?" he asked.

In the short time they had spent together, Molly had found an affinity with Michael, one she had rarely known with anyone else. She felt she could trust him, just as he had trusted her with his grief.

"I left in such a hurry. There is still the matter of my aunt's house, of the inheritance, of what will happen when I return to Wisgate, which one day I must surely do. I do not know if this tale will have a happy ending, even if for now it seems it has," she replied, and he gave her a reassuring smile.

"I think it will—I think you are the sort of person who could do anything if they set their mind to it. Practise is all it takes," he said, and she laughed.

"Now it is you who are helping me," she replied, just as Pollyanna gave a squawk and darted forward to snatch a cake from one plate.

"And after all those crackers I gave her," Michael exclaimed, as Molly scolded the parrot for her rudeness.

"I think we have outstayed our welcome," she said, rising to her feet.

But Michael stopped her, his hand on her arm, their eyes meeting as he smiled at her and shook his head.

"You will always be welcome here," he replied.

***

Molly had a great deal to tell the others when she returned to the campsite later that day. They marvelled at her description of Rowlands Park and asked many questions about the duke and his son.

"Did he really want to learn to juggle?" Bill asked, shaking his head in amazement.

"He wanted to learn everything. I am certain that he will be as good as any of us. He has a true determination—he and his father are coming to see the performance again tomorrow night," Molly replied.

"It does not really change," Algernon said, scratching his head.

"They know that, but they enjoyed it so much they want to see it again—and I might practise something different for them," Molly said, her enthusiasm growing at the prospect of showing off her skills once more.

"Now, Molly—do not get ahead of yourself. There is many a performer who have fallen short in their enthusiasm," Celi warned her, and Molly's face fell.

"I just… he was so upset over his mother, but seeing the troupe perform, I know it lifted his spirts," she said, and Celi smiled.

"Then I am sure it will do so again tomorrow. But come now, we have chores to see to, and Pollyanna needs putting back on her perch," she said, beckoning Molly to follow her.

But for the rest of the day, Molly could not help but be distracted by the prospect of seeing Michael again. She had no friends her own age—her aunt had been her only friend in Wisgate, and the other members of the dancehall troupe were all far older than her. She was looking forward to seeing Michael again, and she was certain that with a little practise he could make his dreams come true, just as she had done, too.

Chapter 12
The London Show

Molly was sad to say goodbye to Michael and the Duke of Thurlstone. They were as good as their word and when she stepped out onto the makeshift stage in the village hall where the following evening's performance was held. Michael's was the first face she saw. He was grinning up at her as Algernon draped the blindfold over her face, and she pictured him as she juggled, smiling at the thought of his own attempts at juggling the day before.

"It was wonderful, Molly–I could not take my eyes off you, I wanted an encore," Michael said, when after the performance he came to congratulate her.

Molly blushed, taking the flowers he had brought for her from the garden at Rowlands Park and smiling shyly at him as they came to the point of farewell.

"I will not forget you," she said, and he shook his head.

"Nor will I forget you. I feel as though we have known one another all our lives. You will come back, will you not?" he asked, and Molly glanced at Celi, who nodded.

"With the rotation of the seasons, and the two of you can write to one another, too–Molly need only tell you where we shall be a week later than she sends her letter," she replied, and both Molly and Michael's faces lit up in delight.

"I will write—and I will tell you of my progress. I promise I will practise as hard as I can," he said, and Molly smiled.

"I know you will—and the next time I see you, you will be able to join me on the stage," she replied.

"I am not sure about that—but perhaps I will keep the balls in the air a little longer than before," he said, still grinning at her.

The Duke of Thurlstone slipped an envelope into Molly's hand and winked at her.

"A little something to aid you on your way," he said, and Molly blushed, realising the envelope contained many pound notes.

"Oh, thank you, your Grace," she said, but the duke only shook his head.

"You have brought us a little light and happiness, Molly, and we shall not forget you," he replied.

Molly knew she would not forget them, either, and after they had bid one another farewell, she felt a sudden pang in her heart, a feeling of sadness at the parting of ways. Celi looked at her and smiled.

"It is the lot of us who travel the roads, Molly. We see so much of the world, but we have no roots to lay down. We stay a while, and sometimes a piece of our heart stays, too. I knew you would realise that one day, as sad as it might seem," she said, and Molly nodded.

"I will not forget him," she said, and Celi put her arm around her.

"And he will not forget you, either, Molly," she replied.

***

But whilst a little of Molly's heart remained in Bath, there was hardly time to dwell on it, for the dancehall troupe was now making its way to London. This was to be the highlight of their year, a performance in a grand theatre with many hundreds of people expected to attend.

"And I want you to be the one who opens the show, Molly. You will go on first and prepare the way for the rest of the performers," Algernon told her, as they rode together towards the capital.

"In front of all those people?" she exclaimed, and Algernon laughed.

"You have done it before, Molly—the size of the audience does not matter. All you must do is what you do when you are alone. You are a natural performer, and you have already proved yourself to be capable," Algernon replied.

Molly was grateful to him for the confidence he showed in her, even if her nerves still sometimes got the better of her. She was excited to see London—her aunt had often told her about the grand theatres and the performances she had seen in Covent Garden and the West End.

"Perhaps I should practise a new act—one with Mr. Marvolo or Celi and Bill and the animals," she said, and Algernon nodded.

"I think that would be an excellent idea, Molly, although Marvolo will not take kindly to interference in his act—you know what he is like. But you and Pollyanna would make a fine double act," he replied, and so it was decided.

They performed in several towns and villages on their journey from Bath to London, but it was the capital on which their sights were set and when at last they came in sight of the dome of Saint Paul's Cathedral and the spires of the city churches, Molly could hardly contain her excitement.

"We are to perform at the Adelphi Theatre on the Strand," Celi said, as the caravans joined the throng of carts, hansom cabs, carriages, and horses, which mingled on the primary thoroughfare into the city.

"I have heard of it—my aunt spoke of it once," Molly replied, gazing around her at the sights of city life.

London was like nowhere she had seen before, an assault on the senses, with hundreds of people bustling back and forth, the air filled with sounds and smells such as Molly had never known before.

"It is one of the most famous theatres in London, and we are honoured to perform there," Bill said.

"Honoured," Pollyanna repeated, for she was sitting on his shoulder.

The procession of caravans had attracted considerable attention, particularly the elephant, who was being followed by a band of street urchins, much to the annoyance of his tamer, a tall, well-built man named Rupert, who flicked his whip at the children, shouting at them to stay back.

"You will have him scared," he cried out, as several of the other performers came to assist him.

Their progress through the city was slow, but at last they arrived on the Strand and to a place where they had been permitted to draw up close to the theatre. It would be a strange campsite that night, and Molly stayed close to Celi and Bill as they unpacked the caravans whilst Algernon entered the theatre in search of a steward to help prepare them for the evening's performance.

"There are so many people," Molly said, glancing around her nervously.

"That is London for you—I lived here a while when I was younger, working as a boot boy, shining gentleman's shoes. The city is a big place, it is easy to be lost in it. Stay close to us, you will be all right," Bill said, and Molly nodded, taking Pollyanna on her arm as Algernon now appeared and beckoned them to follow him.

"The elephant will have to stay outside," he said, laughing, as the keeper tried to pull the animal forward.

"Just like every performance," Rupert complained, rolling his eyes.

They made their way into the grand entrance hall, and Molly marvelled at the sight of the elaborate decorations. Everything was gilded in gold or hung in red velvet. A grand staircase—reminding her of that at Rowlands Park—rose in front of them, sweeping left and right, with signs pointing to the stalls and boxes reserved for the upper classes. A steward in livery stood stiffly in front of them and gave a curt bow as they entered.

"The stage door is at the back of the theatre. You shall enter that way this evening, but it is beholden to offer you a glimpse of the grandeur of your setting," he said in a rather pompous tone.

Molly had to try hard not to giggle. She followed behind as they made their way up the staircase and through a set of large oak doors into the theatre itself. It was a vast, cavernous space, lit by gas lamps, semi-circular in design, and with the stage obscured by yet another red velvet curtain.

"It is so big," she whispered.

"Imagine the audience," Celi replied, and the troupe stood in awe, gazing down at the stage which, in a few hours, they would perform on.

"You will not be disappointed, sir," Algernon said, and the steward looked at him and nodded.

"No, Mr. Trott, we shall not be," he replied.

***

They spent the rest of the day preparing for the performance. Molly, Celi, and Bill practised in a dressing room in the bowels of the theatre, perfecting an act involving Pollyanna sitting on Molly's head as she juggled, and Bill and Celi lifted her into the air. As she practised, Molly's thoughts turned to Michael. She would imagine him in the audience that night, a friendly face amidst a sea of strangers. The thought gave her confidence, and by the evening, they had perfected their act, confident of the adulation they would receive.

"No other dancehall troupe can perform as we do," Bill said, smiling at them both, just as one of the theatre boys came to tell them it was almost time for the performance to begin.

"We have quite a crowd out there tonight—I am told one of the royal princesses is in attendance," Algernon said, mopping his brow as they came to join him in the wings.

"She will be in awe of us," Mr. Marvolo said, and Molly smiled.

She had her juggling balls in hand, and Pollyanna perched on her shoulder. Algernon now stepped out onto the stage with his usual flourish, though that night, Molly had noticed he was dressed in a new suit and top hat, determined, it seemed, to make the right impression.

"Roll up, roll up, roll up, for Algernon Trott's dancehall spectacular..." he began, beginning his oft-rehearsed speech.

"We have practised long and hard–we know what we are doing," Bill said, and Molly and Celi both nodded.

"Yes, and Pollyanna, too," Molly replied, as the parrot flapped her wings.

"Cracker?" she said, and the three of them laughed.

"Only after your performance," Celi replied, tapping the bird's beak, just as Algernon announced their act.

Molly thought of Michael and her aunt. She imagined the two of them willing her on and, taking a deep breath, she followed Celi and Bill onto the stage to thunderous applause. The stage was lit by candles burning in glass surrounds along the front and sides. Molly could not see much beyond the pit in which the orchestra sat ready to play for the performance, but she imagined the hundreds of seats she had early seen, filled with fashionable ladies and gentlemen eager for the performance to begin. The applause died down, and Molly stepped forward, lifting Pollyanna up to perch on her head. Bill was to blindfold her and at their cue, the orchestra was to play so that the three of them could dance as Molly juggled.

"Ready?" Bill whispered, and Molly nodded.

She took the first of the juggling balls in hand, as muted whispers came from the audience beyond.

"One, two…" Celi counted, but as Molly threw the first juggling ball up in the air, a shout came from the side of the stage, and a group of women suddenly burst out from the wings.

"Stop this dreadful act—she is only a child, a poor, exploited child. You should be ashamed of yourselves," the lead woman exclaimed.

She was dressed similarly to Mrs. Mallory, in a long, black dress with a brooch at the neck, her grey hair done up in a bun, and her face set in an angry expression. She was holding a placard which read "The Sin of the Dancehall" and the other women, too, held equally provocative banners.

"Celi?" Molly said, her eyes growing wide with fear as the woman came right out onto the stage.

"It is all right, Molly," Celi said, putting her arm around her.

"It is not all right at all—you should all be ashamed of yourselves. A den of iniquity—bawdy entertainments on the stage, an ungodly display of exploitation. This poor child should be removed at once," the woman cried, as her companions voiced similar sentiments.

Boos and jeers now erupted from the audience, and several items, including a shoe, were thrown at the group of women, who stood their ground even as several of the theatre stewards appeared to haul them away.

"How dare you interrupt our performance," Algernon exclaimed, hurrying onto the stage, his face red with anger.

"It is our Christian duty to do so, we are members of the Dancehall Reform Society, and we make it our business to interrupt those performances in which children are exploited as this poor girl is being," she said, fixing her gaze on Molly, who still had Pollyanna on her head.

"But I want to be here," Molly exclaimed, tears welling up in her eyes as the woman stared at her in horror.

"You do not know what you are saying, child–do you go to school? Where are your parents? How could your family possibly condone such wickedness?" she exclaimed.

"We are Molly's family," Celi said, as still the boos and jeers came from the unseen audience beyond the stage.

"We have paid good money for this performance," a man's voice called out.

"This really is not the place for such a protest," one steward said, trying to usher the protesters off the stage.

"It is just the place for such a protest–the audience must be made aware. This is an ungodly sight, a child exploited, a performance filled with debauchery, and–" she began, but at that moment, Pollyanna took flight from Molly's head, flapping her wings in the woman's face and causing her to scream.

The audience laughed as the protesters now fled from the stage, pursued by Pollyanna, who squawked at the top of her voice.

"Crackers, crackers, crackers!" she exclaimed, as Molly and the others composed themselves.

"Ladies and gentleman, we can only apologise for such a remarkable interruption–I must assure you that all our performers are delighted to find themselves on stage, including Molly, who will now perform her act for you," Algernon said, glancing at Molly who, though feeling somewhat shaken, nodded.

"Well done," Celi whispered, and the performance now began.

But the experience had left an unpleasant taste in Molly's mouth—she worried as to the woman's words, and what would happen if there was further protest. What if these women discovered who she was and where she came from? Perhaps they would even take her back to her father and Mrs. Mallory. The thought sent a shiver running through her, and when the performance was finished, she insisted on returning to the caravan and climbing into bed.

"Why did that woman say I had been exploited?" Molly asked, when Celi came to bed later that night.

"There have been protests before—the dancehall reformers. They think we represent vice, that we are corrupting society, and that children are the victims of such vice," Celi said, blowing out her candle and climbing into bed.

"What will they do? Will they stop me from performing?" Molly asked, fearful of what might become of her if the protests continued.

"They have no real influence—do not worry, tonight was an unfortunate occurrence. We will leave London tomorrow, and we shall not be troubled by them again. They will continue to make noise, but you heard the audience this evening. They loved your performance, and we know the truth—you love to perform, too," Celi replied.

But despite her reassuring words, Molly could not stop herself from worrying. She was anxious at the prospect of what might become of her, and having left so many of her worries behind, it seemed the past was catching up with her.

"I will not go back," she vowed to herself, even as the possibility seemed uncomfortably close.

Chapter 13
Hiding in Plain Sight

"I am afraid it is the only way, Molly. Heaven knows it is not my choice, but these… women, with their high morals and loud voices… they would have us disbanded if they could," Algernon said, shaking his head sadly as they rode with Celi and Bill on the board of the animal's caravan.

It was the following day, and Molly and Celi had awoken to the sounds of a commotion on the street outside the caravans in front of the theatre. The women, with their placards and banners, had returned, accompanied this time by a fiery mouthed clergyman–quite the opposite to the affable Mr. Crockford–who stood loudly denouncing the dancehall as a sin against God and the triumph of the devil.

"Be ye warned, tis' hell which awaits ye," he cried, pointing his finger as Molly and Celi opened the door to their caravan.

"Crackers! Crackers," Pollyanna squawked, but the seriousness of the situation was clear for all to see.

"How many times must I tell you? Molly is happy here with us. We do not force her to do anything she does not wish to. It was she who came to us," Algernon said, but his reply fell on deaf ears, and it was only after they had packed up their things and set off in a dejected procession along the Strand that the cries of the protesters were subdued.

"And I am never to be allowed to perform again?" Molly asked, tears welling up in her eyes at the thought of being denied the happiness she had grown so used to in the months gone by.

"Not in front of an audience—not until your age makes it so that we are not accused of cruelty," Algernon replied, sighing, and fixing her with a sorrowful look.

The news was like a dagger to the heart. Molly's only desire was to perform, to show off her skills to an audience, and to hear their adulation—it had made her so happy, and now that happiness was denied her.

"You can still practise, Molly, and you can help with the animals, and fetch and carry for the performances. You will still be part of the troop, but until this sorry business is passed, we cannot risk further protests. These women have a great deal of support, and it will only take a few of them to ruin us," Celi said, putting a sympathetic arm around Molly, who brushed the tears from her eyes.

Molly knew she was right. The protesters had vowed to make their message heard, and to give them further ammunition for their protest would only strengthen their resolve. If they discovered more about Molly, and her father learned of where she was, then her happy life would be over, and she would be returned to Wisgate and all the misery she knew awaited her.

"I loved being on stage," she replied.

"And you will be so again, but not until it is safe for us all," Algernon said, jumping down from the board to urge the others on behind.

They were making their way slowly out of the city, the hustle and bustle of the centre now giving way to the outlying slums. Soon they would leave London behind, returning to the peace of the countryside, but the legacy of their time there would remain, and Molly knew she would not appear on stage alongside Celi, Bill, and Pollyanna until her age gave her the freedom to do so.

"But what am I to do until then? Am I to live entirely on your good will?" Molly asked, and Celi smiled.

"You are one of us, Molly, and we take care of our own. Besides, you can teach us a thing or two, I am sure. There is no one else that can juggle with a blindfold on, let alone with Pollyanna perched on their head. We could all learn from you," Celi replied.

But though her words offered some comfort, Molly knew that the years to come would pass slowly, her dreams shattered by the sadness of what had occurred.

"I will still follow my heart, Aunt Sally," she said to herself, as they left London behind and struck out into the unknown once again.

***

"I have something here that will cheer you up, Molly," Celi said, entering the caravan one morning a few weeks later.

Molly was sitting on her bunk repairing one of Mr. Marvolo's costumes. He had torn the seam at the shoulder, and she had almost finished stitching it up, when Celi came hurrying in, holding a letter in her hand.

"For me?" Molly asked, laying aside her sewing and looking up in surprise.

"Someone postmarked it from Bath. It must be from Michael," Celi replied, and Molly leaped to her feet and hurried over to take the letter from Celi's hand, tearing it open and reading.

"It is from Michael," she exclaimed, reading it through rapidly, a wide smile coming over her face.

"What does he say? Is he well?" Celi asked.

"He is very well, and he writes to say that he has been practising his skills every day. He can now juggle with three balls and stand on one leg whilst doing so–though he admits to falling over frequently as he attempts it," she said, her heart filled with delight at receiving Michael's news.

She had written to him in the sad aftermath of their experiences in London, lamenting her sorry lot and telling him of her determination to continue practising, even if she could no longer perform.

"He must be sympathetic to your plight, Molly," Celi said, and Molly nodded.

"He writes he feels terribly sorry for me and wishes there was something he could do. He even jokes that he will ask his father to build a theatre for the two of us at Rowlands Park and that we shall perform there to our heart's content, and with no silly women to protests against us," she said, feeling suddenly both happy and sad to read his words.

She was happy to have a friend like Michael, albeit at a distance, one who understood her as she understood him, their shared sorrow—and shared delights—forming a bond which would only grow stronger, and sad because in that moment, she dearly wished to see him and discuss the matter properly.

"Perhaps one day, he will. He will be Duke of Thurlstone in years to come, and then he may build a theatre as big as he wishes," Celi replied.

"I would like that," Molly said, reminded of the theatres she and her aunt would create with upturned packing cases and chairs from the dining room at Rosedene.

"I am pleased you have made a friend like Michael. The two of you barely had a chance to know one another, but you formed a bond so strong, and with your letters, too," Celi said, putting her arm around Molly and kissing her.

She had become like a sister to Molly, as kind to her as anyone had ever been. The two of them had grown close in the months since Molly's unexpected arrival, as close as any sisters might be. Molly trusted her, and she was grateful to her for her words, words which brought her comfort despite her sorrow in that moment.

"I only hope I will see him again soon—not only when we return to Bath. Do you think I will?" Molly asked, and Celi sighed.

"I cannot promise you it, Molly. But I hope so, truly, I do," she replied.

Celi now went to see to the animals, and they left Molly alone with the letter, reading it repeatedly and imagining all the things she would say to Michael if he were there with her now. She pictured him in the drawing room at Rowlands Park, the housekeeper despairing of the near misses to the Ming vases as Michael practised his juggling skills. It made her smile to think of him, and she wished he was there now, the two of them practising together and growing closer.

"I am sure he will keep practising," she said to herself, and forgetting all about Mr. Marvolo's ripped shirt, she sat down to begin her reply, telling Michael everything she could think of, and encouraging him in his newfound skills.

***

"One, two, three, and jump," Molly said, just as Bill fell flat on his face, the twirl of the skipping rope wrapping around his ankles, the juggling balls flying in every direction, one narrowly missing Celi who ducked and laughed.

"Oh, it is no good. I shall never get the hang of it," Bill complained, shaking his head as he stooped down to pick up the errant juggling balls.

"You just have to concentrate and jump as the rope passes over your head," Molly replied.

They had been practising an elaborate new act for much of the morning, one in which Bill would leap over a skipping rope whilst juggling at the same time. The intention was eventually for him to be blindfolded, but they had made such little progress that Molly feared only the easier part of the act might be accomplished. For her, such a feat proved easy, and she had already demonstrated it four times with Celi and Bill holding the skipping rope as she leaped up and down, juggling four balls at once.

"You make it sound so simple," Bill said, as Molly stepped forward to show him once again.

"Watch—you just need to count. One, two, three, jump, one, two, three, jump," she said, as Celi and Bill swung the piece of rope around.

Molly now juggled, counting as she went. It was the way she did all her tricks – counting to a rhythm and ensuring she did precisely the same thing at the same time each time.

"You are better than any of us, Molly," Celi said, staring at Molly in amazement.

"I just... know how to do it," Molly replied.

It was hard to explain, like riding a bike or learning to swim. There had been a time when she could not do it, and now she could. She thought back to the first time she had held a set of juggling balls, unable even to throw one into the air without dropping it. Now, it was second nature to her, like breathing or walking. She did not have to think about it—she did it, and that was that.

"And how we wish you could do it on stage. Algernon will not be happy if we do not do something new," Bill said, as Molly now handed him the juggling balls and took the end of the skipping rope from him.

"It is all I wish, too," she replied, and Bill sighed.

"I know it is, Molly. I am sorry, I was not thinking. We all of us wish you were back with us on stage. It is not the same without you, and Pollyanna is acting up terribly. It takes three crackers before she will as much as utter a squawk," he said, shaking his head.

"Only a few more years to go," Molly said, trying to sound cheerier than she felt.

"And until then, we must settle for falling flat on our faces like a pair of clowns," Bill complained.

"Then we must keep practising," Molly replied, knowing that she herself needed to do so, too, determined to ensure that when the happy day came, she was ready for it.

Part Three

Chapter 14
Home Again?

The days passed, and the years passed, and Molly grew used to her life in hiding. She cooked and cleaned, sewed and mended, wrote to Michael, and practised her skills at juggling and magic. They encountered no more protests, but Algernon was careful to keep Molly away from prying eyes, and during the performances she would always remain hidden in the wings, watching and never allowed to take part. She was eighteen now and had lived in this way for six years, patiently waiting to perform again and realise her dream of being on stage.

"I can hardly believe I managed it," Bill said, slumping down into a chair outside the caravan after the evening's performance.

It was high summer, and the troupe had just performed in a small village on the borders of Bedfordshire. Their route had taken them north for the past two years, and prior to that, they had performed in East Anglia and Lincolnshire. But now they had journeyed south again and were close to Wisgate, where they were due to perform in a matter of days. Molly had been growing increasingly nervous at the prospect. For now that her eighteenth birthday had passed, Algernon had promised she might perform on stage again.

"You managed it very well," Celi said, as she placed Pollyanna on a perch outside the caravan which she and Molly still occupied together.

"And with my eyes closed. It is quite remarkable. But I did what you told me to do, Molly–what you have always told me to do–I counted," he said, and Molly laughed.

"That is the way to do it, Bill. Just count and everything else will come naturally. That is the way my aunt taught me," she replied.

Bill had mastered a difficult trick, one that Molly had been trying to teach him for several months, and that evening had seen its debut on stage. He had performed it perfectly, and both Molly and Celi had been extremely impressed.

"We can do it together in Wisgate," Molly said, and Celi and Bill glanced at one another with raised eyebrows.

"Molly… we have been meaning to talk to you about that. Do you really think it wise for your first performance to be in Wisgate after all these years? You must surely be terribly nervous about returning there. What if–" Celi began, but Molly interrupted her.

She had thought long and hard about the possibility of performing in Wisgate. This was something she had to face, even though she understood their concerns. She was no longer a child, but had surely proved herself a woman, and to cower in the face of her father and the memories which returning home had roused would be to admit defeat.

"I have to face it. I cannot shy away from the truth of what lies before me. I will not do so. I have waited too long. I will show them–and they will get a surprise when they see me. The entire village will," she replied, imagining the gasps when she stepped out onto the stage.

She knew nothing of what others believed her fate to have been. She had heard nothing of the happenings in Wisgate, nor of her father's search for her–if indeed there had even been such a search. As far as she was concerned, she had been given up for lost–a runaway, expected never to return.

"There are many memories there, Molly–memories you have not confronted in many years, and you haven't stepped out on stage since you were twelve years old. Won't you reconsider?" Celi asked, but Molly shook her head.

"I've considered it, Celi, I've got to do it," she said, picking up a set of juggling balls and idly tossing them up in the air.

Celi and Bill exchanged glances once again, but Molly ignored them. She knew her own mind, and she had expressed her thoughts and worries to Michael in a letter. He had written back to encourage her, and that had been all she had needed to give her the confidence to proceed. She would not hide away from her past, nor shy away from confronting her future.

"We just want what is best for you, Molly," Bill said, and Molly smiled.

"I know you do, but this is something I have to do. Not only for myself, but for my aunt, too," she replied.

***

The caravans arrived on the outskirts of Wisgate a few days later. Their appearance caused the usual excitement which greeted them wherever they went, and many of the local people came to view the elephant, who acted as a draw for the ticket sales which took place on the day before the performance. Molly stayed hidden in her and Celi's caravan, watching out of the window for anyone she might know. She recognised Mr. Crockford, the curate, who came to buy his ticket accompanied by a small boy—presumably his son—who seemed hardly able to contain his excitement at the prospect of the performance. Molly smiled, imagining the look on the clergyman's face when she stepped out on stage.

There were others, too, whom she recognised, though she saw no sign of her father or Tobias in the queue for tickets. She remembered his words about frivolity and imagined the look on his face when he discovered the dancehall troupe had returned to the village. He would shake his head and offer a curt dismissal. But she knew their arrival would bring back memories for him of the last performance in Wisgate and of the events surrounding it.

"We sold all the tickets," Celi said, when evening had come and the last of the villagers had left the campsite.

"I am looking forward to performing," Molly said, for she had been practicing long and hard for what was to come.

Her new act involved juggling and singing. She would dance, too, and perform magic tricks—perfected through many long hours of practise. She was excited to perform again, even as her nerves were growing greater with every passing moment.

"And you are sure you want to?" Bill asked, but Molly was adamant she was.

"I have to," she said, folding her arms and fixing her two friends with a resolute expression.

No one would persuade her to the contrary, and later that evening, when the others had gone to bed, Molly slipped away from the campsite through the dark streets of the village and made her way towards Rosedene. It felt strange to be back in Wisgate. It was all so familiar, and yet different, too. Molly was different. She had grown up, no longer a child, but a woman. She was not afraid of her father anymore, and as the cottage came into view, she paused, remembering her aunt, and how she had so often protected her from her father's wrath.

"And I have returned," she said to herself, slipping through the garden gate and looking up at the outline of the house, which was silhouetted in the moonlight.

The garden was overgrown, a mass of brambles and briars. The trees had grown taller, the branches hanging down almost to the roof of the cottage. Molly caught herself on a thorn, the wound smarting, and she stumbled, falling flat on her face with a cry.

"Oh, goodness me," she exclaimed, scrambling to her feet, and catching her skirt on another thorn, the material ripping as she did so.

Molly smiled to herself—this was the garden's way of chastising her for its neglect. Her aunt would be horrified to see the neat order she had so diligently maintained reduced to a mass of thorns and weeds.

"I wonder..." Molly thought to herself, and she made her way over to the potting shed, pulling the door opened with a rusty creak.

She could see the outlines of her aunt's gardening tools, and there amongst them was a pair of shears. To an observer, it would have seemed like madness, but Molly was gripped by a sudden desire to restore order to the garden—if only a tiny part of it. She took down the shears, which, to her surprise, had not rusted in the years since last they were used, and fought her way back through the brambles, chopping at anything she could reach until at last she had cut a way through the garden to the arbour which had once been her aunt's pride and joy.

It was there she and her aunt would sit, and her aunt would regale Molly with stories of the past, and of her many adventures in far-flung places abroad. The seat was broken now, but in the moonlight, Molly could see the white roses growing up around it, forming an arc of perfumed protection above her. She perched on the edge of the broken seat, thinking of her aunt, and smiling to herself at the thought of what she would say if she could see her now.

"You must perform, tomorrow, Molly," she would have said, and Molly breathed in the sweet scent of the roses, which reminded her of her aunt's perfume.

One day, she vowed to reclaim Rosedene—the rightful inheritance her aunt had left her. She would clear the garden and make it once again a place of beauty and refuge. The thought pleased her, and she closed her eyes, imagining the cottage as it had been when she and her aunt would spend their days there happily together.

"You always believed in me," she thought to herself, remembering her aunt's words once again.

"Always follow your dreams, Molly, always follow your dreams…"

Chapter 15
Performance
of a Lifetime

The excitement in the village was palpable, and all day, a steady stream of curious spectators came to gaze at the caravan. They kept the elephant keeper busy with the attentions of small boys daring one another to touch the noble creature, who stood patiently tethered to the trunk of a large oak tree. Molly, Celi, and Bill spent the day practicing their act, even as Molly made several foolish mistakes, her nerves overtaking her as the hour of the performance grew nearer.

"Oh, for goodness' sake," she exclaimed, dropping the juggling balls for a third time.

She had practised this act so many times without fault, but today of all days, she simply could not manage it.

"I told you this was a bad idea," Bill said, and Molly gave him a withering look.

"I am just… preoccupied," she said, and Celi and Bill exchanged what had now become a familiar look.

"You must not push yourself, Molly. You should wait and perform in the next village," Celi said, but Molly shook her head and picked up her juggling balls, determined to try once again.

"I will not be kept hidden any longer," she said, and taking a deep breath, she threw the balls into the air, this time catching them without any dropping to the ground.

As evening approached, the troupe made its preparations for the performance. Mr. Marvolo was suffering from a sore throat, but he insisted to Algernon that the show must go on, and together the performers made their way to the church hall, where a large crowd had already gathered in anticipation.

"Do you recognise anyone, Molly?" Algernon asked, for he, too, had had his doubts as to Molly performing that evening.

"Some of them, yes–the curate is here with his wife, but I do not see my father," she said, peering out through the stage curtain at the audience.

Some seats were yet to be occupied, and there was still time for her father and Tobias to appear, even as Molly doubted they would. Tobias would be a young gentleman now, and she could only imagine how insufferable he must have become in the years since last she had set eyes on him.

"Do you want to see him?" Algernon asked, and Molly turned to him and sighed.

A part of her never wanted to see him again, whilst another part desired to prove herself in his eyes. She was not the girl who had left Wisgate all those years ago, and she was not afraid of the man who had done so much to make her life a misery.

"If I do, then so be it," she replied, as the time for the performance now came.

Molly stood in the wings, watching as Algernon stepped out on stage to begin his welcoming speech. It could have been a night like any other, the same as hundreds which Molly had witnessed in the years she had been with the troupe. But tonight was different. Not only was she to perform after years in the shadows, but it was to be her homecoming, too. Her father—whether or not he was present—would soon come to know of it, and whether or not he approved, he would see that Molly had made a life for herself beyond the strict confines he had once imposed.

"Roll up, roll up, roll up, for a spectacle like no other. We present to you, the fire eater, the magician, the acrobats and performers, the jugglers, and dancers—all for your excitement and delectation," Algernon said as the musicians played, and the audience applauded.

"Are you ready, Molly?" Bill whispered, and Molly nodded.

It twisted her stomach in knots, her hands trembling, her nerves rising—but she thought of her aunt, imagining her to be in the audience with a smile on her face, urging Molly on.

"I am," she replied, and together, the three of them stepped out onto the stage.

***

Since she had left Wisgate, they had fitted the church hall with gas lamps, the gentle, flickering glow from which illuminated the audience below. Molly recognised the curate and his wife, along with several others–farmhands and other labourers, all of whom looked up at her in surprise and astonishment, whispering to one another, as she appeared on stage. There was a short musical interlude, during which Molly, Celi, and Bill were to prepare their act, but Molly's eye was now drawn to the front row of the audience, on which, to her horror and amazement, sat several recognisable figures.

"Molly, the juggling balls," Bill whispered, but Molly could not take her eyes off the front row, transfixed by the sight of her father, Tobias, Mrs. Mallory, Michael, and the Duke of Thurlstone all sitting next to one another, oblivious, it seemed, as to whom they were sitting next to.

All of them were staring at her, three with animosity and two with rapture. She did not know whether to laugh or cry. Michael and the duke would have not understood to whom they were sitting next to, and neither would her father, Mrs. Mallory, or Tobias, know anything of Michael or the duke. It would have seemed funny if it were not so terrible.

"I..." she began, her father's gaze cutting through her like a dagger.

"You must," Celi hissed, and summoning all her courage, Molly suddenly leaped up into her performance.

She was perfect and did not make a single mistake for the entire duration of the act. She sang and danced, juggled and performed, imagining her aunt to be cheering her on. When the performance was over, the three of them took a bow, and Molly caught Michael's eye, smiling as he leaped to his feet with rapturous applause.

"Bravo!" he called out, and to her amusement, he threw a red rose onto the stage in appreciation.

But whilst the rest of the audience was on its feet, three figures remained resolutely still–her father, Mrs. Mallory, and Tobias–who had grown into a portly young man with a red face and was wearing an ill-fitting yellow waistcoat, white shirt, and breeches.

"Was that…?" Celi said, as they made their way offstage.

"My father, my brother, and Mrs. Mallory, the housekeeper," Molly said, sighing, even as she felt elated in the aftermath of her performance.

"Do you think they will speak to you–and the duke and his son, too?" Bill said, shaking his head in amazement.

"I do not know," Molly replied, as Mr. Marvolo hurried past them through the wings and out onto the stage.

The church hall at Wisgate was hardly a grand venue and with no dressing rooms, the troupe had made do with wheeling two of the caravans round to the yard at the back to have a place to change between the acts. Molly, Celi, and Bill made their way outside, glad of the cool evening air after the heated exuberance of the performance. But Molly's mind was elsewhere. She could think only of Michael, of her father, and the others. Michael had not indicated that he intended to surprise her in this way. He had grown into quite the handsomest of men, but she would have recognised him anywhere, still with that same kindly smile and twinkling eyes. So many years had passed since last they had been together, and yet it felt like only a moment, her heart beating fast at the prospect of his seeking her out, even as she knew her father would, too.

"A wonderful performance, quite spectacular," Algernon said, appearing in the yard when the performance had ended.

"And Molly was the star of the show," Bill said, smiling at Molly, who could not help but feel proud of herself for having at last stepped out on stage once again.

"We look forward to even greater things, we…" Algernon said, but a shout from behind interrupted him.

"Molly! What is the meaning of this?" her father's voice echoed across the yard, and Molly turned to find him, Mrs. Mallory, and Tobias advancing towards her.

"Father, I–" Molly began, but her father, his face flushed with anger, grabbed her by the arm and dragged her towards him.

"Gone runaway, we gave you up for dead. How dare you repay us in this way? It humiliated me tonight. But I had a feeling, yes, I thought you would be with them," he exclaimed, shaking her, as Tobias laughed.

"Foolish sister," he said, pointing at her and jeering.

"You wicked, child," Mrs. Mallory exclaimed, but Molly pulled away from her father's grip, and stood facing the three of them defiantly.

"I am not a child any longer, and I will not be spoken to like that by the Mallory woman," she cried, echoing her aunt's name for the housekeeper, who now stared at her in speechless disbelief.

"You… all of you. What is this?" her father cried, turning to look at the other performers, who had now come to stand at Molly's side.

"I would ask you the same question, sir," Algernon said, and the others nodded.

"We know all about you. We know what you did to Molly. Bill rolled up his sleeves and said, "We know the sort of man you are."

"Strike him, Father, box his ears," Tobias exclaimed, jumping up and down behind Molly's father, pointing at the performers and jeering.

But as he spoke, a flap of wings rose from the dark caravan behind, and Pollyanna swooped towards him, her talons outstretched, cawing ferociously.

"Crackers! Crackers," she exclaimed, and Tobias turned pale, falling back with a cry as Pollyanna dived on him and sent him rolling onto his back, wailing like a baby.

"She only wants a cracker," Celi said, and the rest of the troupe laughed.

"You leave Molly alone. Can you not see she is happy here? Besides, she is her own woman, she makes her own decisions. What say you, Molly?" Mr. Marvolo said, and Molly nodded.

There were tears in her eyes, but they were not tears of sorrow or fear. She had nothing to be afraid of now. Her father held no sway over her, nor did Mrs. Mallory. For the first time in her father's presence, Molly felt a sense of power, and she fixed him with a defiant gaze and folded her arms.

"I am not going anywhere. And what is more, you will give me Rosedene, and my aunt's inheritance. You have no right to keep them from me," she said, even as her father's face turned red with rage.

He spluttered, reaching down, and dragging the wailing Tobias to his feet, before pointing his finger angrily at Molly and cursing her.

"You will get nothing," he cried as Mr. Marvolo and Bill advanced towards him.

"I think we have heard enough from you tonight, sir. Off with you," Mr. Marvalo said. And faced with the performers, Molly's father had little choice but to turn tail and flee.

"You have not heard the last of this, Molly," he called back as he, Tobias, and Mrs. Mallory fled.

"What horrible people. They say the apple never falls far from the tree. But I would say you were grown from a different tree than that, Molly," Bill said, turning to Molly and shaking his head.

Molly's hands were trembling, but she smiled at Bill, turning to the others to thank them.

"He is not my father—in name, perhaps, but nothing else. You are my family, and you have proved that tonight," she said, just as another set of footsteps came hurrying across the yard from the church hall.

"Molly!" Michael exclaimed, and Molly turned to find him with beaming face and arms outstretched, coming towards her.

He embraced her—much to her surprise—and now the others melted away, leaving the two of them alone.

"I... I was not expecting you. Why did you not tell me you were coming?" she asked, still astonished by the sight of him standing there before her.

He was no longer the boy she had first known in Bath, just as she was no longer the girl he had known, either. They had grown up, but their affection for one another had not diminished. If anything, it had grown stronger. He took her hand in his, their eyes meeting in a gaze of mutual understanding. She blushed, shaking her head, and laughing in disbelief.

"I... I know it is foolish. But when you wrote and told me you would be in Wisgate, and that you would perform again for the first time tonight... I had to come. I had to see you," he said, and he brought her hand to his lips, kissing it, his face etched with a look of such loving affection as to make Molly's heart skip a beat.

"You were sitting next to my father," she said, sighing and shaking her head.

"I heard him talking to the woman about you-that must be the fabled Mallory woman you spoke of. I did not like to say anything, but the things they were saying... they quite appalled me," he said.

"That is their way, I am afraid. My brother, too. I have not seen them in all these long years, and yet they are just the same as they ever were-cruel and unforgiving. My father will not give up Rosedene, nor will he ever acknowledge the inheritance which is rightly mine. I can do nothing," she replied, and she sat down on the steps of one caravan and put her head in her hands.

Michael sat down next to her, and he put his arm around her shoulders. She rested her head against his, and, for a few moments, they sat in silence, familiar enough for that silence not to matter. She was grateful to him for making such a journey to be with her, but even as she delighted in his presence, she feared his company would be all too fleeting.

"There must be something we can do, Molly. Have hope. My father's lawyers can look into the matter, and—" he began, after they had sat a while together, but Molly interrupted him.

"But you will go back to Bath. You cannot stay here," she said, turning to him with a puzzled expression on her face.

"But did I not promise to practise all you taught me?" he asked, and she raised her eyebrows curiously at him.

"To juggle?" she asked, and he nodded.

"Yes, and more. I have not come just to watch and then slip away. Molly, I do not want that. I want to perform. I want to join the troupe!" he said, and at these words, Molly gasped.

Chapter 16
Difficult Decisions

Molly and Michael sat talking long into the night, and Celi had to drag her away as the church bell tolled midnight. Michael was staying with his father at the inn on the village green, and he walked with them as far as the lychgate, the two of them arranging to meet the following morning. But that night, Molly could barely sleep, her mind racing with thoughts of all which Michael had told her.

"Oh, Molly, can you not keep still? Every time you roll over, the caravan creaks and I am woken up," Celi said, striking a match and lighting the candle in the alcove of her bunk.

Molly sat up, rubbing her eyes and yawning.

"I cannot sleep. So much has happened this evening. It is all going around in my head. My father, the performance, Michael," she said, and Celi swung her feet over the side of the bunk and jumped down to the floor.

"Shall I make us some cocoa?" she said, and Molly smiled and nodded.

"I do not think I will sleep tonight," she said, and Celi sighed.

"Then cocoa it is," she replied.

The stove was soon lit, and water boiled-the caravan filled with the sweet scent of the cocoa. Molly wrapped herself in a blanket and sat on a chair opposite Celi, who had cut a piece of gingerbread for them both, before handing Molly a steaming cup with a smile. She had lit the oil lamps, and the caravan felt warm and snug, even in the dead of night.

"It surprised you to see Michael. I could tell you were," she said, and Molly blushed.

"I did not expect him to come all the way from Bath just to see me," she admitted.

"And why not? The two of you have written to one another almost every week for the past six years. Did you not think he might have affection for you?" Celi asked.

Molly blushed even further. She considered Michael her closest friend–a strange fact given they had been in one another's company only once. But that bond of friendship had only strengthened in the years since their first encounter, and Molly knew Celi's words to be true. Her affection for him grew only stronger, and with his astonishing words of that evening ringing in her ears, Molly could only imagine what the future might hold.

"Well... I suppose so, but... he is talking about joining the troupe. He is the son of a duke, and yet all he seems interested in is performing. He wants to juggle and dance and act and sing. Tomorrow, he is going to perform for me. But he cannot possibly remain with us," she said, even as the possibility seemed eminently attractive.

"And why not? Did we not accept you, too? Anyone is welcome. We are all outcasts, Molly, we are all looking for something else. Duke or pauper, there is a place for everyone here," Celi replied.

Molly nodded. But it was not just the question of Michael's arrival which perplexed her. Returning to Wisgate had roused many feelings in her and seeing Rosedene again for the first time in so many years had made her wonder as to the future. Her aunt had left her the house, along with a substantial inheritance. It was rightfully hers, and her aunt would have been horrified to think that Molly's father had taken that right away from her.

"I am... not sure if I will carry on," she said, even as the words seemed astonishing to repeat.

She had spent so long waiting for the chance to perform once again that the thought of stepping back, of doing something different, seemed absurd. But Molly could not rid herself of the thought that something else was calling her to remain. This was a fight she had to win, otherwise her father would forever have a hold over her. She had to fight back, and to save what her aunt had worked so hard to build.

"Are you... are you saying you will not come with us?" Celi asked, her eyes growing wide.

"I am not sure. But there is something here I have to do. I have told you about Rosedene, about the gardens there, and about my aunt's inheritance. Coming back here has... made it all seem to matter once again," she said, even as she felt confused as to her conflicting feelings.

"But Molly... the act... you cannot possibly want to give that up," Celi said, a note of astonishment entering her voice.

Molly sighed. Celi was right, she did not want to give it up. But neither could she bear the thought of leaving Rosedene behind, either. Her heart was torn, and with Michael's appearance, Molly knew she had a terrible choice to make.

"I wish for both, but I cannot have both. I can choose only one and that is that. You must believe me when I say it is the hardest of decisions," Molly replied, taking a sip of cocoa.

Tears welled up in her eyes, and she sighed, shaking her head as she thought of all they had shared. Celi was like a sister to her, and the troupe was her family. Life with the dancehall was all she had known, and she wondered what her aunt would have said, had she been there to offer her advice.

"Follow your dreams, Molly. Always follow your dreams," Molly could hear her saying.

But in that moment, Molly's dreams were conflicted. They were neither one, nor the other. She thought of Rosedene, with its overgrown gardens and long hidden memories. Could she restore it? Reclaim it? The possibility filled her with anticipation, but to do so would be to leave behind another dream—if only for a short while.

"You must do what you think is right, Molly. But… I will miss you terribly," Celi said, and she set aside her cup of cocoa and rose to embrace Molly, tears rolling down her cheeks.

"It need not be forever. But I must see to my affairs here. There is still so much left undone. When I left, I was a child, but now I am grown up, and I cannot allow my father to win. I will not be controlled by him anymore," Molly said, and she clung to Celi, trembling at the thought of what she was about to do.

"There will always be a place for you here, Molly, and we shall always be your family," Celi replied.

They sat a while longer, finishing their cocoa before climbing back into their bunks and settling down to sleep. But Molly remained restless, and she was glad when the first rays of dawn broke through the curtains, and the time came to rise and see to the animals.

"I have decided," she told Celi, as Pollyanna squawked for her crackers.

"And what had you decided?" Celi replied.

"I am going to stay. I am going to fight this battle, and I am going to win," she replied, a look of resolute determination coming over her face.

***

"Stay behind?" Michael exclaimed when Molly had explained her plan to him later that morning.

They had met in a sitting room behind the parlour of the village inn, where Michael and the duke had taken lodgings. Michael had come early to the campsite to seek her out, keen to show her the fruits of his years of practise with the juggling balls. But Molly had insisted they went somewhere to talk, and over cups of strong coffee, she had made clear to him her desire to remain in Wisgate and claim Rosedene as her own.

"I know you must think me terribly foolish," she said, but he shook his head, even as a look of disappointment came over his face.

"Not at all. But... I suppose I was a fool to think it. I imagined joining the troupe, of performing together, of travelling across the country to thunderous applause," he said, and Molly smiled.

"But you could go. Celi and Bill, and Algernon, Mr. Marvolo–they would all welcome you with open arms," she said, but Michael shook his head.

"It is you I wanted to be with," he admitted, blushing as he averted his gaze.

"I... but why, Michael?" she asked, even as she knew the answer.

"Because... we can do as we please now. We are not bound by the rules of others. I wanted to be with you, I wanted to perform together, and now..." he said, his words trailing off.

Molly feared she had upset him, and she reached out and took his hand in hers, squeezing it as she spoke.

"I know you are disappointed, but you can still perform. I am not holding you back," she said.

"I want to stay with you. I know it is foolish–I dragged my father halfway across the country to watch your performance. I have acted rashly, I know that. Might I... might I show you what I have learned?" he asked, and she smiled at him and nodded.

"I would like that very much," she said, and he grinned at her, rising to his feet and holding up his finger.

"One moment, I must bring the juggling balls," he said, and he hurried out of the room, returning a short while later with a box, which he placed on a table in the corner.

"And you have really practised all this time?" she asked, watching him with interest as he prepared to perform.

"Did I not say as much in my letters? I have practised every day–night and day. You do not know what this means to me, Molly. But I want to promise you something–I will stay with you until this sorry business is at an end. I would like to see Rosedene, and I would like to learn more about your aunt. She sounds the most remarkable of characters," he said, and Molly smiled.

"I would like you to stay, too," she replied, and now he turned to her with a flourish, tossing the first of the juggling balls up into the air.

He caught it, and Molly clapped, as now he threw up a second, and a third, catching them in rhythm, counting as he went.

"One, two, three–just as you taught me," he said.

Molly watched in surprise. She remembered the last time she had seen him attempt to toss the juggling balls into the air. But there was no doubt he had been practising. Now he closed his eyes, and to her astonishment, he turned, juggling as he went.

"How are you doing that?" she exclaimed, and he laughed.

"It is all in the counting–one, two, three," he said, still turning as he juggled, and the balls surrounded him like a whirlwind.

With a last flourish, he caught them, opening his eyes, and taking a bow. Molly leapt to her feet and ran to embrace him.

"Oh, it is wonderful, Michael! I cannot believe what you have achieved," she said, gazing up at him with a smile on her face.

"I did it for you, Molly. You do not know how you have helped me in these years gone by. When my mother died, it was as though my entire world had collapsed. I had nothing, and my father was similarly afflicted, inconsolable with grief. We were like ships without a rudder. But you brought the wind, Molly, and you helped me grasp my grief and overcome it. I cannot thank you enough," he said, and she nodded, knowing that his friendship, too, had meant the same to her.

"We both know the pain of loss and what it is to be close to someone, to love them, and to feel their absence. We're kindred spirits," she said, and he smiled at her, tossing one ball up into the air for her to catch.

"And that is why I had to come. No one else can understand as you do. They think this is all a mere frivolity, but to me… it is life," he said, and Molly smiled.

"I do understand, and that is why I shall only stay here for as long as is necessary to set my aunt's affairs in order. I will catch up with you. You can take my place in the show. When Algernon sees you perform, he will have no qualms in your becoming one of us," she said, but Michael shook his head and laughed.

"But Molly, I cannot go without you. I am going to stay. We will fight this together. Your father will not win, and together we can restore Rosedene to the glory you once knew. Do you not see... I came here to be with you. That is all," he said, and Molly breathed a deep sigh of relief, thankful to him for all he had done for her.

At that moment, the door to the sitting room opened, and the landlord—whom Molly recalled was named Samuel Peterson—showed in the Duke of Thurlstone, offering him his thanks for patronising his humble inn.

"Yes, thank you, Landlord," the duke said, with a twinkle in his eye.

"And if there is anything your Grace or your Lordship requires, please ask," the landlord said, bowing to the duke, who was trying hard not to laugh.

"Yes, thank you. I am sure we will," he said.

"Actually, Father. There is something this good fellow could do for me," Michael said, and the landlord's eyes lit up.

"Name it, sir," he said.

"Lodgings for the coming weeks. I will remain in Wisgate a while longer than expected. And a room, too, for the young lady. Two rooms, one for me, one for her, and a sitting room where we might take our meals. But there is one stipulation, Landlord," he said, and the landlord nodded.

"Name it, sir?" he said, even as the Duke of Thurlstone looked somewhat perplexed by this unexpected news.

"That no one—especially the residents of the grange and the manor, should know of it. We will keep ourselves to ourselves," he said, and the landlord fell into such a deep bow that Molly feared he might topple forward.

"You honour me, sir... your Lordship. We will do all as you instruct," he said, but Molly shook her head.

"You may lodge here, Michael. But I shall stay at Rosedene. I have the key, and... well, there is something comforting about the thought of being close to my aunt," she said.

The duke now demanded an explanation, albeit in his usual affable manner, and Michael explained his intention to remain with Molly and do all he could to assist with her plight in securing Rosedene and her aunt's inheritance.

"Goodness me, I knew your father to be a cruel man, but I did not know you had suffered so terribly at his hands, Molly," the duke said, shaking his head.

"We must be able to put a stop to this, Father. Could you speak to your lawyers in London?" Michael asked, and the duke nodded.

"The stipulation of a will is very clear. If a legacy is left, then that legacy is the right of the named recipient. Your father may have claimed wardship over your inheritance in the past, Molly, but he should have no right to do so now. Although... the matter of a woman's property is tricky. Your aunt was a woman of independent means, but you are still your father's responsibility until marriage. I will look into the matter," he said, and Molly thanked him profusely.

She knew there would be a great upset of her friends in the troupe, and that Celia and Bill, in particular, would be distraught to learn she was not coming with them. But Molly knew she was doing the right thing by remaining behind–not only for herself, but for her aunt's memory, too.

"Then all that remains is to say goodbye," she said, and Michael put his arm around her and squeezed her.

"We will do it together," he said, and she smiled at him, grateful for all he had done for her, and for all he was yet to do.

Chapter 17
Parting is Such Sweet Sorrow

"Here is the route we shall be taking. You could catch up with us at any time," Algernon said, thrusting a map into Molly's hands as the troupe prepared to depart from Wisgate the next day.

She had never seen him cry before, but the tears were rolling down his cheeks, and he shook his head, holding up his hands as though he could hardly bear the thought of their parting.

"And we will catch up, I promise. It will not be long," she said, as the others now came to offer their heartfelt condolences at this sad parting of ways.

"I hardly know what to say," Mr. Marvolo said.

"It is strange for you to be lost for words, Marvolo," his assistant said, raising her eyebrows.

"You are a part of this family, Molly. And I never taught you to eat fire," Mr. Marvolo said, shaking his head as he took Molly by the hand.

"You still can. This is only farewell, not goodbye. As soon as we settle things here, I will follow you," she said, and Mr.

Marvolo nodded, turning away, as Celi and Bill came forward to embrace her.

"Pollyanna will miss you, too. You always gave her extra crackers," Bill said.

The parrot was sitting on his shoulder, and she seemed to sense the goodbye, her head cocked to one side as she cawed.

"Come home, come home," she said, and Molly laughed.

"I fear I have two homes, Pollyanna. One here, and one with you. I cannot remain in both," Molly replied, reaching up and stroking the parrot, who now let out a mournful cry.

"Then we must hope you soon visit us," Celi said, and she put her arms around Molly and kissed her on both cheeks.

"I will, I promise," Molly said, and now the troupe climbed into the caravans or took up the reins of the horses, and prepared to depart.

Michael, too, saw them off, and the two of them watched as the elephant was untethered and led to the front of the procession. A band of village children watched, and there was much cheering and clapping as the troupe made its way through the village and onto the road leading east.

"Goodbye, dear friends," Molly whispered, as Celi and Bill waved, and Pollyanna flapped her wings.

"You will see them again very soon," Michael whispered, and he put his arm around her, the two of them now standing along on the village green.

Molly took a deep breath, knowing that a monumental task lay before her. The thought of facing it alone had filled her with dread, but to have Michael at her side, and to know he was to remain there through whatever trials and tribulations she would face, filled her with renewed hope.

"We both will," she said, slipping her hand into his, as a new future now lay before them.

***

"And this is where I gave my first performance. Just here," Molly said, pointing to a patch of bare grass on which now lay a great pile of cuttings from the trees which grew overhead.

"It must have been a magnificent garden," Michael replied, pulling out a handkerchief and mopping his brow.

The two of them had spent the afternoon at Rosedene, cutting back the brambles and clearing the lawn. They had barely made an impact, so overgrown were the gardens, but Molly was determined to see Rosedene restored to its former glory, knowing how proud her aunt would be if she could only see her now.

"It was the most beautiful place in the world," Molly replied.

She knew it was a foolish thing to say–beauty lay all around her, and on her travels through England with the dancehall troupe, she had seen many wonderful sights. But there was something about Rosedene, the memories it evoked, the past it held… This had always been her refuge, and, amidst the sorrows which life had once held, the gardens, the house, and the comforting presence of her aunt had been for her a soothing balm against the ugliness of the world she had known.

"There is something magical about it," he said, setting down a pair of shears and gazing up into the trees above.

"I know what you mean–I feel so safe here. It was always the same. My aunt's house was a place to escape to. I knew I was welcome here, just as I was with the dancehall troupe," she said, looking around the gardens, every corner of which brought forth fresh memories for her.

"Your aunt must have been a most remarkable character," he said, and she turned to him and nodded.

"I wish you could have met her–just as I wish I could have met your mother. I hope I am like my aunt, and I am sure you are like your mother, too," she said.

Michael sat down on a tree stump, and Molly came to sit next to him, reaching down and plucking at the daisies which grew like a carpet all around.

"My father always says I take after my mother. Not so much in looks, but in my ways and in my mannerisms. She was a very determined person, and I hope I am like her, too," he replied.

"It takes a good deal of determination to learn the skills you have learned," Molly said, and Michael blushed.

"I wanted to do it for you, too. I made you a promise all those years ago, and I am glad I have fulfilled it," he said.

They sat a while beneath the dappled shade of the trees. The garden seemed to embrace them, a warm breeze blowing gently through the banks of wildflowers which had grown up all around, perfuming the air with a sweet scent which reminded Molly of her aunt's perfume. Everywhere she looked, her aunt's spirit seemed to rest, and it felt to Molly as though the house itself was welcoming her home.

"You will perform, I promise you. We will restore this house and the gardens, we will find a way to claim the inheritance, and then–" she began, but an angry shout from the lane lcut her words off.

"Trespassers! Trespassers! Be on your way!" a man was shouting, and Molly leapt to her feet, angry at such an interruption.

"I beg your pardon! I think you will find that it is you who are trespassing if you take a single step further into this garden," she exclaimed, glaring at at the man who now stood at the garden gate.

She did not recognise him from the past. He was an elderly man with a red face and white hair, shabbily dressed, and carrying a pair of shears in one hand, his other raised with a wagging finger.

"His Lordship has made it his business for me to tend the gardens here. The house belongs to Master Tobias," he said, opening the gate and stepping through.

"Now just you wait a moment," Michael said, stepping forward, but Molly was not afraid, and she strode forward towards the man, pointing her finger back at him.

"You may tell *my father* that "Master Tobias," has no claim on Rosedene, and that if he wishes to dispute the matter, then he may come and talk to me about it," she said.

The man looked at her in surprise and scratched his head.

"Your father?" he replied, sounding puzzled, and Molly gave a curt nod.

"Yes, do you not know who I am?" she asked, and it seemed the man did not.

"This is his Lordship's property. I tend the gardens and see to the house. You have no right coming here… you wait until his Lordship hears of this," the man said, but Molly only laughed.

"If they charged you with tending the gardens, then you have left them in a sorry state–that much is certain. And you should know that my Aunt Sally left the house and gardens to me. This is my house, and my garden, and I would ask you to leave," she said, placing her hands on her hips and facing the man defiantly as Michael stood at her side.

"You have not heard the last of this, his Lordship will–" the man began, but it was Michael who now interrupted him.

"His Lordship may come and speak with us, and he shall have a shock when does," he said, and the man now muttered something under his breath and turned on his heels, marching out of the gate and closing it so hard behind him that one hinge broke.

Molly sat down with a sigh.

"What a thoroughly unpleasant man," she said, putting her head in her hands.

She knew there were battles ahead, and that her father would stop at nothing to prevent her from claiming what was rightfully hers. She could still not understand his deep-seated animosity towards her. He had his heir in Tobias, and she knew that with her cousin's ailing health, the title of Baronet would soon pass to her brother. There was no reason for his spite, except for the very fact of a terrible hatred, the likes of which she may never fully understand. It grieved her to imagine what her mother would think, and what her aunt would say if she could have witnessed the scene which had just played out in the garden of Rosedene, the house which was Molly's by right and inheritance.

"I fear we have not seen the last of him–and he is certain to bring your father here," Michael replied.

"Let them come, we shall be ready for them," Molly replied, and with a grim determination in her heart, she took up her discarded shears and set to work, eager to see the garden returned to its full splendour and once more become the happy refuge she had once known it to be.

Chapter 18
The Battle for Rosedene

Despite Michael's insistence to the landlord that his presence, and that of Molly, remain a secret, it was not long before word spread through the village that the daughter of Lord Walden–as Molly's father liked to style himself–had remained behind in Wisgate in a bid to reclaim Rosedene. All manner of speculation had arisen following her disappearance, including the suggestion she had been kidnapped by the dancehall troupe, but now she had returned, the residents of Wisgate were curious as to her intentions, and a steady procession made its way to the garden gate of Molly's aunt's house, peering across the garden hoping to catch a glimpse of her.

"They are there again–the two sisters," Michael said, peering out of the parlour window.

Molly rolled her eyes and came to stand next to him, gazing across the garden, which was now largely cleared of brambles, and to where two women stood looking over the garden hedge.

"They were here yesterday. I think their name is Spalding, two elderly spinsters–keen on gossip, I believe," she said, and she pulled the curtain across the window and laughed.

Molly had found no difficulty in getting into the house on the day the dancehall troupe had left the village. The key was just where she had hidden it and found it again on the night before the performance when she had first returned to Rosedene. The house had been neglected. It was dusty and filled with cobwebs, but everything was still in its proper place, and between them, Molly and Michael had soon cleaned and swept the parlour, where a fire now burned merrily in the hearth. The butterfly collection had remained in pristine condition, and the two of them had spent many an hour over the past few days marvelling at the sight of the specimens inside the glass cases, all of them labelled in Molly's aunt's neat handwriting.

"I would love to see some of these butterflies in flight," Michael said, crossing to one case and peering down into it.

"Perhaps one day you shall. There are so many adventures to be had. My aunt kept meticulous journals. They are all there on the shelves," Molly said, pointing to the bookcases which lined the far wall of the parlour.

"She had remarkable courage, truly remarkable," Michael said, shaking his head.

"She was a remarkable person, she–" Molly began, but a loud banging on the door interrupted her, and startled, she turned to Michael with wide-eyed fear.

"Let me answer it," he said, and he made his way to the door, pulling back the bolt and opening it cautiously.

Molly came to stand behind him, and over his shoulder she could see her father, along with Tobias, the white-haired man who had accosted them from the garden gate, and another gentleman she did not recognise, who was wearing a top hat and tails, a large moustache covering his upper lip.

"I want to talk to you, Molly," her father said, putting his foot in the door.

"And what is it you want to talk to Molly about?" Michael asked, standing between Molly and her father.

Molly's father looked at him with disdain, his eyes narrowing.

"You were at the performance the other night. Who are you? What is it you want with *my* daughter?" he demanded.

"I am Lord Michael Dickens, son of the Duke of Thurlstone, of Rowlands Park near Bath," Michael said, drawing himself up.

Molly could not help but smile. She knew Michael sat lightly to his title and would never normally have used it to such an effect. In his letters, he would often speak of how he hated the trappings which rank and wealth brought him, and that airs and graces meant nothing to him. But at this moment, the effect was just what was needed. Molly's father's eyes grew wide with surprise, and he glanced at the others even as he tried to assert himself. Molly knew her father craved those same trappings which Michael detested. He had always been angry at playing second fiddle to his brother and believed the title of Baron should have been his. But to come up against a man who would one day become a duke now seemed to unsettle him, and he stammered his response as the others looked worried, too.

"And... and what is you want with my daughter? What business does the son of a duke have in staying in a run-down old house like this?" he demanded.

"I am lodging in the village. I would not presume to remain here and cause scandalous rumours to develop. But Molly and I have been the closest of friends for many years, and I have made her a promise to remain by her side until this sorry business is resolved. Now, say what you have to say, or forever hold your peace, sir," Michael replied, and Molly could not help but be impressed by the manner in which he spoke.

"Troublemakers, both of you, but... well... this is Mr. Edmund Cartwright, my lawyer, and he is here to tell you that a legal challenge is to be mounted against your so-called inheritance, Molly. This house, and your aunt's legacy, belongs to me. It is to be held in trust for Tobias until he comes of age, though I doubt he will have need of it himself owing to the title which is to be his," her father said.

Molly glanced at Tobias, who stared back at her with a smirk on his face. He was becoming more like their father with every passing day. She could not help but feel sorry for him, even as she knew he possessed few redeeming qualities.

"And on what grounds do you mount this challenge, sir?" Michael asked, addressing the lawyer, who now cleared his throat.

"On the matter of wardship, my Lord. Miss Walden may have—in progressive views—come of age, but she is still her father's ward, that is, until she is married. This house, her aunt's legacy, all of it, legally belongs to her father," he said, raising his eyebrows.

"We shall challenge such assertions. You are not the only one who knows the law, Mr. Cartwright. My father's lawyers are–" Michael began, but Molly's father interrupted him.

"Your father's lawyers are what? What business is it of yours? What has Molly done for you to make you so loyal? I detect the whiff of scandal here. An unmarried heir to a dukedom cavorting with a dancehall chorus girl. The scandal papers will have a field day, my Lord," Molly's father said, and he and Tobias laughed.

"Why must you be so cruel?" Molly demanded, and she stepped past Michael and pulled the door open wide, facing her father with a defiant gaze.

"Because I never wanted you, Molly, and I see no reason you should profit from my sister's foolishness. That is why," he replied, and Tobias now jeered at her.

"You were not wanted, you were not wanted–go back to your parrot and your silly friends," he said, sticking his tongue out at her.

"Those silly friends are worth a dozen of you, Tobias, and I shall go back to them–oh yes, they are my family. More so than any of you have ever been. This is my house, my aunt left it to me, and the legacy, and I am no one's ward– whatever the law might say," Molly replied, and she turned and slammed the door in their faces, even as her father shouted after her in an angry voice.

"This is only the beginning, Molly, only the beginning," he said, and now their footsteps could be heard retreating along the garden path.

Tears welled up in Molly's eyes, and she sighed, slumping down into a chair by the fire and shaking her head.

"Do not worry, Molly, my father's lawyers will fight this. We will not give up. Rosedene is yours. It is what your aunt wanted," he said, as Molly looked up at him with fear in her eyes.

"But he is right. I am my father's ward—we cannot go against the law. I feel so helpless, even as I know what you say is true. My aunt wanted me to have Rosedene. She wanted me to be free of my father," she said, as Michael came to put his arm around her.

"And you will be, Molly. Have faith," he said, but faith was in short supply for Molly, who knew she was close to losing everything, even as she tried desperately to cling to her aunt's memory, and the inspiration she had left behind.

"I want to make the garden beautiful again," Molly said, turning to Michael, who smiled.

"Then we shall. We will clear it and plant it, tend it, and watch it grow," he said, rising to his feet and clapping his hands together.

Molly forced a smiled. She knew he was trying to cheer her up, even if she felt far from cheerful in the wake of what had just occurred.

"But what is the point in restoring Rosedene if my father is only going to take it and hand it over to Tobias?" she asked, shaking her head sadly.

"But he is not, Molly—I assure you of that," Michael replied, and there was such certainty in his voice that Molly could not help but find hope in what he said.

"I do not understand," she replied, but he only took her by the hand and pointed through the window out into the garden beyond.

"We shall make it a performance, Molly—the garden is a theatre, the plants and trees our actors and musicians, and we—we are the artists," he said, hurrying her towards the door and out into the fresh air.

The two of them stood breathing in the sweet fragrance of the gardens, which seemed, as Michael had promised, poised for something new. Molly looked around her, overwhelmed by what lay ahead, and yet with a determination to salvage something, anything, from that which her aunt had gifted her.

"Perhaps we can," she said, feeling Michael's infectious enthusiasm, even as the future weighed heavily on her, and she wondered if she was strong enough for the task which lay ahead.

***

"Look, Molly—the roses are budding," Michael said, pointing up to where a host of flowers had appeared on the arbour above them.

The scent was fragrant, filling the garden with a delightful perfume. Michael reached up and plucked a single rose from amongst the thick foliage, which had burst into bloom with the early morning sun. He handed it to Molly, who raised it to her nose and smiled. The flower was of a deep, velvety red, and she smiled at him, gazing around at the garden, which seemed to burst more into life with every passing moment.

"It is beautiful," she said, sitting down on the arbour and gazing out across the lush green lawn beyond.

It was three days since Molly's father had delivered his ultimatum, and Michael and Molly had spent every waking moment in the garden, so that the encroaches of nature were cut back, and it had been restored much to its former glory. It had seemed to Molly as though the garden had lain in a deep slumber, waiting for her to return. It was slowly waking up, now, raising its beautiful head and smiling at them in thanksgiving for this fresh burst of life. Everywhere she looked, the plants and flowers were reappearing in all their glory, so that every shade of colour imaginable seemed to be before them, sheltered by the trees which arched their boughs overhead, framing the garden like a portrait in which she and Michael had placed themselves as the protagonists.

"And it will only grow more beautiful yet," Michael replied, smiling at her.

"It is a paradise. I cannot believe how quickly it has returned to what it once was. I can just picture my aunt sitting beneath the willow tree, and the stage we once constructed for our performances," Molly said.

She could see it all so vividly, remembering so many happy memories, and everything she and her aunt had shared in that beautiful place.

"It only took a short while. Imagine what it can become," Michael said, rising to his feet and offering her his hand.

"Only for my father and Tobias to take it. What will they do with it?" she asked, shaking her head sadly.

Molly could only imagine what would become of Rosedene in the hands of her father and brother. They would not love it, they would not care for it, and they would allow the garden to be overcome by nature, a tangle of brambles and thorns, just as she had found it on her return to Wisgate. The thought made Molly feel sick, and she sighed, turning to Michael, who was looking at her with a smile on his face.

"It does not have to be that way, Molly," he said, and she looked at him curiously.

"But what do you mean? How can it be any other way?" she asked, and to her amazement, he now sank to one knee in front of her, taking her by the hand and gazing up at her with eyes wide with longing.

"Molly, I did not come to Wisgate only to see you perform. I came because... because I love you. I know it must seem foolish, but you are my dearest friend, even though we have barely spent a week in one another's company. All those letters, the intimacies and joys we have shared–it has all meant so much to me. I love you so very much, and I cannot imagine being happier than in a life shared with you," he said, his gaze fixed on her, his hands trembling as he held hers in his.

"Do you... do you mean it? This is not merely an act of charity, is it? I cannot accept if you feel obliged to do this for me. We will find a way, your father's lawyers–" she began, but he shushed her and shook his head.

"No, this has nothing to do with charity, Molly, only with love. But if you do not feel the same, then... yes, we will find another way. But if you can find it in your heart to love me, then marry me, and we shall be happy here at Rosedene together all the rest of our lives," he said, even as she knelt before him and threw her arms around him.

There was no doubt in Molly's mind that she loved him—that she had always loved him ever since that first moment she had set eyes on him, watching her with rapturous delight in the audience at the Bath theatre. She loved him for his kindness, his joy in life, for all they had shared, for his determination, and for his protection of her. She loved him with her whole heart and to marry him would be the greatest joy and delight she could imagine.

"I will marry you, of course, I will marry you," she exclaimed, and he sat back and gazed at her in delight, clutching her hands in his and bringing them to his lips.

"Oh Molly, how happy you have made me! You do not know how happy I am to know your feelings for me are the same," he exclaimed, and he leaped to his feet, jumping up in the air with delight.

Molly laughed, rising with him as the two embraced once more.

"Did you think I would refuse you?" she asked, and he looked embarrassed.

"I did not know—perhaps you would have done. I wondered if perhaps I had misread your feelings for me—all those letters, the things we told one another, the feelings we shared. But my own are certain. I have loved you all these years gone by, and every letter you sent me caused me to fall more in love with you than ever. My heart feels light as a feather, I could sing and dance for joy," he said, and, as though the garden had heard him, a gentle breeze now blew through the trees, rustling the branches and bringing a burst of scent from the flowers.

Michael and Molly twirled together across the lawn, and he hummed as though they were amid a waltz, the two of them dancing between the flower beds, delighting in the perfect moment they now shared.

"I could not feel happier than I do now," Molly said, as they came to a halt by the garden gate, turning to look back at the house which could now be their home.

"But I want to promise you something, Molly. Your aunt's inheritance is yours. Forget all this nonsense about wardship and property. I will not have it. Rosedene is yours, and if you wish to live here, then we will," he said, and Molly smiled at him and squeezed his hands, gazing into his eyes and seeing that smile reflected in the look he returned her.

"But one day you will have a great responsibility. You will be the Duke of Thurlstone and will have the magnificent estate of Rowlands Park to preside over," she said, and Michael sighed.

"But how I would long to remain forever here with you, where life is simpler. Do you know something? I have always envied your freedom, the freedom to come and go, the life you led on the road. My own life felt so constricted compared to that," he said, and he leaned forward and kissed her on the cheek.

"But sometimes I envied your life, too. The safety of certainty, your loving father, all of that. My aunt always taught me to live in the moment God gives you—the flight of a butterfly, the scent of a rose, the warm breeze on your face. Perhaps, for now, we can live in that moment, and think nothing of the future which lies before us, wherever life might take us," Molly said, resting her head on his chest.

"I think I would like that–and I would like to think we could live in every moment God gives us. Oh Molly, we have so much to look forward to, even if there are trials still lying head," he said.

They stood for a moment in silence, the perfumed breeze wafting over them, the birds singing in the trees, and the garden surrounding them in the same embrace with which they held one another. Molly could not have felt happier in that moment. She thought nothing of the past and nothing of the future–only of the happy joy which was theirs.

"My father will be furious when he discovers what we have done," she said, as the two of them now made their way back inside the house to make tea.

"Let him be, and I want to propose something further– that we make no delay in getting married. We can go to the curate immediately–tomorrow morning–and he can marry us and Rosedene will be yours," Michael said.

Molly's eyes grew wide with amazement at the possibility which lay before them. It seemed too incredible for words. Marriages were things which were planned. They took months to organise and yet... there was no reason to delay. She nodded and the two of them embraced, sharing a kiss as Molly's heart seemed fit to burst with happiness.

"Then we shall soon be man and wife," she whispered, and he smiled at her and nodded.

"And there can surely be no greater happiness for us than that," he replied.

Chapter 19
A Secret Revealed

When Molly and Michael called at the rectory the next morning, the curate, Mr. Crockford, received them in his study. He had been making a study of certain scholarly texts but appeared only too happy to be interrupted by those who could talk with him about the delights of the dancehall, and Molly and Michael were received enthusiastically into the study, a large room lined with books which looked out onto a rose garden – another of the curate's many hobbies.

"I am sure there are some who would accuse me of conduct unbecoming to a clergyman in attending the performances, but they are my chief delight," he told them, as his wife served them with tea and drop scones spread liberally with butter and jam.

"I am glad you enjoyed it, Mr. Crockford," Molly said, taking a sip of tea and glancing at Michael, who smiled.

"Enjoyed it? Oh, it was the most wonderful spectacle. The fire eater, Mr. Marvolo, he is quite remarkable, and you, Molly, oh you were wonderful. And yet you have remained in Wisgate. I cannot for the life of me think why?" he said, raising his eyebrows at her.

Molly blushed. Her misfortunes at the hands of her father and Mrs. Mallory were not common knowledge in the village. To many, her life at Wisgate Grange must have seemed idyllic, and they must have wondered why she had run away in the manner she did. But if the truth were known, her father's reputation would be mud, and he would find little support from the likes of Mr. Crockford and the other villagers.

"Rosedene–my aunt's house," she replied, and the curate looked at her in surprise.

"But Rosedene belongs to your father. It is to be in your brother's inherit, along with the title of Baronet," Mr. Crockford replied.

Molly glanced at Michael, who gave her a reassuring nod.

"The truth is quite different, Mr. Crockford," Molly replied, and she explained to the clergyman the strange circumstances of her childhood and all that had led up to the moment which had brought her and Michael to his study.

"Good Lord, I can hardly believe it," Mr. Crockford replied.

He had uttered a similar invective at several moments as Molly gave her explanation, and it was true. The story was far from believable, even if every word she spoke was the truth.

"Molly is speaking the truth, Mr. Crockford. She has been terribly treated, but we are to set the matter straight, if you will permit it," Michael replied.

The clergyman looked at him in surprise.

"But as tragic as the story is, what can I do to be of service to you both?" he asked.

Michael reached out and took Molly by the hand, and a smile broke over the clergyman's face.

"We would like to be married—but in secret, as far as possible. Molly's father cannot know. Not yet, at least. He would never give his permission, and we are certain he would try to prevent the marriage. But once we are wedded, Molly's property, her inheritance, will revert to me—and I certainly do not want it," Michael said.

Mr. Crockford took off his glasses and brushed a tear from his eyes.

"My dear Molly, how sorry I am I realised nothing of your suffering, and what a noble deed this is by this fine young man. I will marry you. Happily, I will. My wife will serve as witness, but… I wonder," he said, stroking his chin ponderously.

"You do not think we are doing something wrong?" Molly asked, and Mr. Crockford laughed.

"Wrong? What is wrong with love, Molly? No, what is wrong is the terrible ordeal you have suffered at the hands of your father—an ordeal no child should ever have been put through. I will marry the two of you, and all will be well. I am certain of it," he replied.

Molly and Michael left the rectory in high spirits. They had set the date for the coming Thursday, and it being Monday, they had only a few days to prepare. But, as Mr. Crockford had reminded them, all that mattered was love, and there was no doubting that Molly and Michael were in love.

"And when we are married, we shall go straight to your father and make our demands known—a renouncing of

Rosedene as the inherit of your brother and the return of your rights over your aunt's inheritance," Michael said, as they hurried through the village.

"And then we shall re-join the dancehall troupe?" Molly asked.

Michael turned to her, his eyes wide with a look of hopeful anticipation.

"If only for a while... perhaps not forever, but... to perform on stage, to perform together, it would be a dream come true," he said, and she smiled at him and nodded.

Molly had always known it was Michael's ambition to perform. His letters had always spoken of such a dream, and having seen his skills with the juggling ball, Molly was under no illusion that he was ready.

"Then we shall. It will amaze Celi and Bill when they discover we are married," she replied.

"Would you prefer them as guests at the wedding? We could wait, I suppose..." he began, but Molly shook her head.

"I want for nothing except to marry you," she said, just as a jeering voice came from behind them.

"Still here, are you?" it said, and Molly turned to find her brother, Tobias, sneering at them from outside the butcher's shop.

"Wisgate is as much my home as it is yours, Tobias," Molly replied.

She had always tried to be kind to Tobias, though she was certain he would never have forgiven her for locking him in the laundry cupboard on the day of her escape from Wisgate Grange. But the way he was, the person he was, the manner in which he behaved—all of it resulted from his upbringing, and Molly knew that things could have turned out differently indeed if their lives had been reversed.

"Father wants you to leave, and I think he is right," Tobias said, pointing his finger at them both.

He was dressed like a gentleman, but his manner was far from gentle. He was the very image of her father, a bully, and a sneak. Molly could only feel sorry for him, and she shook her head, turning away, even as he continued to taunt them.

"I want nothing to do with you, Tobias," she called back, but he hurried after them, jabbing Molly in the back.

She turned to find his sneering face inches from hers.

"Rosedene is mine, and I will have that horrible garden removed. I will not live there, of course. I will live at the manor house once we can get rid of Cousin Harold. It will not take much," he said, and Molly shook her head in disgust.

"What sort of man do you think you will become?" Michael demanded, but Tobias only laughed.

"And I suppose you are the one who is to be a duke, are you? Well, why not return to your dukedom and stop following my sister around? She has nothing, you know. If you are sniffing around her for an inheritance, then you will find she is as poor as a church mouse. She will have to join up with those travelling performers again before long. My father will have her thrown out of Rosedene—you mark my words," he said, folding his arms and sneering at them both.

"You are very certain of yourself, Tobias," Molly said, shaking her head.

"I know I am right," her brother replied, and still smirking, he turned on his heels and marched off along the street.

"What a horrible child he is," Michael remarked, offering Molly his arm as the two of them returned to Rosedene.

"Alas, I believe there is little hope he will grow into a better man," she replied, even as her brother's words had brought with them a stronger resolve to do all she could to see Rosedene restored.

***

A woman's wedding day should be the happiest of her life, and when Thursday came, Molly knew the day would be just that, even as the thought of celebrating in their own company made her feel a certain sense of sadness. She was unsure where the dancehall troupe would be performing and could not share the joyful news of her betrothal with those she counted as family. The Duke of Thurlstone, too, could not attend, for he had returned to Rowlands Park, and so the wedding was to be witnessed by only the curate's wife and Mr. Crockford himself.

Molly had found a dress which had belonged to her aunt in one cupboard at Rosedene. Despite the years, it was still in good condition, and she had washed and pressed it. She stood admiring herself in her aunt's dressing room mirror, imagining what she would say if she could see her now. Molly knew her aunt would have been the happiest of people on that day, and she imagined her there with her, gently encouraging her and telling her how pretty she looked.

"You have followed your dreams, Molly," she would have said, and Molly smiled at the thought.

Michael would be readying himself at the village inn and with the clock on the mantelpiece striking ten O'clock, Molly had half an hour to walk into the village and make her way to the church. She felt nervous, filled with trepidation as to what was to come, even as she knew she was doing the right thing. She felt happy–happier than she had ever felt–and with a last glance in the mirror, she took a deep breath, knowing that the next time she stood in the parlour of Rosedene, it would truly be hers.

"Come now, be brave," she told herself, and she took up her shawl and brushed the tears from her eyes.

She missed her aunt terribly and would gladly have given up her entire inheritance if only it could have been her who would walk her down the aisle.

***

The lychgate was open and Michael was waiting for Molly, dressed in a frock coat and tails, a yellow cravat at his neck and his hair combed back. He looked terribly handsome, and Molly hurried up to him, throwing her arms around him in delight.

"Oh, Michael, I have hardly slept a wink thinking of this moment," she exclaimed, and he laughed.

"I was pacing the floorboards at some ungodly hour. The landlord brought me a brandy, but it still did not help me sleep. Ah… here is Mr. Crockford and his wife," he said, pointing to the church door, through which had just emerged the surplice clad clergyman, followed by his wife, who was wearing a red dress and matching hat.

"Molly, you look beautiful. Come now, all is ready, though I have one small surprise for you," he said, beckoning them both to follow him into the church.

Molly glanced at Michael with surprise, but he only looked confused as to the possibility of what that surprise might be. The church was an ancient building, dedicated to Saint Nicholas, and the bell was peeling out a merry ding-dong, even as the organ struck up its chord. It seemed strange to attend a wedding with no guests, especially one's own, and, as Molly and Michael stepped inside, she tried to imagine what it would be like to have the entire dancehall troupe in attendance.

"Can you imagine the elephant and Mr. Marvolo here?" she asked, and Michael laughed.

"It would be quite a sight," he replied.

But as they came to the top of the aisle—the two of them intending to walk arm in arm to the front together—Molly noticed a solitary figure standing with his back to them at the front of the church.

"Who is that?" she whispered, and Mr. Crockford turned to her with a smile.

Your cousin, Harold," he replied, and Molly's eyes grew wide with astonishment.

She had not seen the Baron in years, and she had assumed him to have retreated even further into his reclusive nature. But now, as they approached, he turned to them and smiled. He was a pale-looking man—sickly—and Molly realised she had not seen him since the day of her aunt's funeral. But his eyes were bright and keen, and he dressed well, if somewhat eccentrically, in a purple smoking jacket and shoes with sparkling diamante buckles. He was not at death's door as her father had imagined, and Tobias had hoped. She smiled at him, curious to know what had brought him here to witness their happy moment.

"Mr. Crockford has explained everything to me, Molly. How terrible for you! I have shut myself away these long years past, but to hear of your plight... it quite broke my heart," he said, and he pulled a large, spotted handkerchief from his pocket and blew his nose.

Molly smiled and reached to put her hand on his arm.

"You were not to know. My father kept his behaviour as secret, and I know you have had... your own problems," she replied.

Her cousin gave a weak smiled and nodded.

"I have, but they are small compared to your own. But none of that matters now—I am the Baron, and I will see that justice is done," he said.

"What do you mean?" Michael asked, but the Baron waved his hand.

"No, no... now is not the time. Mr. Crockford is here, and he was waiting to perform the marriage," he said.

The clergyman was standing in front of the communion table, his prayerbook open, and he smiled as Molly and Michael came to take their places in front of him.

"It is rarely I perform a wedding without a congregation," he remarked as his wife took her place next to Molly's cousin.

"But I think we have all we need, Mr. Crockford," Molly replied, and the clergyman nodded, clearing his throat as he began the ceremony.

"Dearly beloved, we are gathered together here in the sight of God, and in the face of this Congregation, to join together this man and this woman in holy Matrimony; which is an honourable estate, instituted of God in the time of man's innocency, signifying unto us the mystical union that is betwixt Christ and his Church…" he said, as Molly and Michael stood before him, arms joined, each as happy as the other.

***

Molly and Michael made their vows in an almost empty church, with only Harold, Mrs. Crockford, the bell ringer, and the organist to act as witnesses. But despite the sadness of absent friends, Molly knew she could not have been happier when Mr. Crockford pronounced them husband and wife. Molly turned to Michael, and he put his arms around her and kissed her, even as the curate's wife clapped and cried.

"Oh, I am always a nervous wreck at a wedding," she said, pulling out her handkerchief and dabbing at her eyes.

The Baron, too, congratulated them and, with the final blessing given, Molly and Michael walked arm in arm up the aisle and out of the church.

"We are husband and wife," she whispered, as though saying it out loud made it real.

"And I hope you feel as happy about that fact as I do," he replied.

She nodded, resting her head on his shoulder as the two of them stood at the church door together. It was a bright day, and several of the villagers, attracted by the sound of the bells, stood at the lychgate for a glimpse of the happy couple.

"Miss Molly, can it be you?" one woman exclaimed, and Molly smiled, a blush coming over her cheeks.

"It can, Mrs. Talbot," she replied, recognising the woman as one of her aunt's old friends.

But at that moment, another familiar figure stepped forward. It was Mrs. Mallory, dressed all in black and carrying a wicker basket in hand. She stared at Molly and Michael in amazement, her mouth half open, her cheeks flushed with anger.

"What is the meaning of this?" she demanded.

"I think it is quite clear what the meaning of this is, Mrs. Mallory," Michael said, even as Mrs. Mallory stepped forward, pointing her finger angrily at them both.

But Molly was not afraid of the housekeeper anymore. She was beyond her cruelty now, and she faced her defiantly, proud to have at last escaped her clutches.

"We are married, Mrs. Mallory. Michael and I are married, and we could not be happier than we are at this moment," she said, her arm still slipped into Michael's, drawing courage from her newfound happiness.

"Married? Without your father's permission? Wicked child!" the housekeeper exclaimed.

"But I am not a child anymore, Mrs. Mallory. I have grown up, and I will not be addressed as if I am still seven years old and at the mercy of your palm," Molly replied.

The other women started whispering amongst themselves, and Mrs. Mallory drew herself up defiantly.

"You always were a disobedient little wretch," she said, turning on her heels.

But at that moment, two more figures appeared at the lychgate—Molly's father and her brother, Tobias. News of the wedding had spread fast, and her father now rushed towards them, panting, his face red with anger.

"How dare you, Molly, how dare you!" he cried.

Molly was about to reply with the same defiance she had used in reaction to Mrs. Mallory, but it was her cousin, Harold, who stepped between them, causing Molly's father to stop dead in his tracks.

"And how dare you, Uncle?" he said, folding his arms and staring at Molly's father with a defiant gaze.

"You… what are you doing here?" Molly's father demanded.

"I am witnessing my cousin's wedding to the future Duke of Thurlstone, which is more than can be said for her own father," Harold replied.

Molly was astonished at the sight of her cousin standing up to her father in such a way. She could not help but admire him, and it was clear her father was just as surprised as she. He stared at Harold in disbelief, even as Tobias jeered at him.

"What do you know about it? Go back to the manor and leave us alone," he exclaimed.

"How dare you speak to me like that? I am the Baron, the head of the family, and I know all about you, Tobias. The way you speak of me as though I am at death's door and as though your inheritance is assured. But let me tell you something—it is not. You will never be the Baron of Wisgate, and what is more, I am turning you out of the grange," he said.

He spoke in such a calm and collected manner that at first, his words did not seem to sink in. Molly's father looked at him in bewilderment, and even Tobias was silenced, the look on his face turning to astonishment.

"You... what?" Molly's father demanded.

"You heard me. The grange is part of the Wisgate estate. I am the Baron and you are my tenants. The whole thing is perfectly clear. I have heard how you have treated Molly all these years, and the manner by which you hold me in contempt. I may be a recluse, but I am not stupid, Uncle. You will have one month to leave Wisgate Grange—I am sure there are cottages in the village where you might take up temporary residence, although I suppose I own them all... Ah, well, another village, perhaps. And what is more, I assure you, the line will not pass to Tobias on my death—in however many years that might be. You have no immediate right to inheritance, especially when you have deprived your own daughter—my cousin—of what is rightfully hers. Rosedene, and my aunt's inheritance," he said.

The confrontation had brought a small crowd to gather at the lychgate, but Molly's father now found his voice, and he let out a loud and angry exclamation.

"Nonsense, it is all nonsense. I shall have you sent to the asylum. You are quite mad. Rosedene is mine, it is—" he began, but now it was Molly who interrupted him.

"But Father, I am no longer your ward. I am married to Michael, and what is mine is his. He is the rightful owner of Rosedene, just as my aunt's will stipulates it should be," she said, hardly able to control the delight she felt at this remarkable victory.

Her father's face had turned purple with anger now. His fists were clenched, and he was shaking, even as it was certain he was defeated.

"But what is more, I do not want it. It belongs to Molly, and I will not stand in the way of her happiness. Rosedene is hers, as is the inheritance," Michael said, and he offered Molly his arm, the two of them stepping forward as a cheer went up from the gathered crowd.

"Thank you, Harold," Molly whispered, and her cousin smiled.

"I know all about the dancehall troupe–I juggle myself, you know," he replied, and Molly shook her head in astonishment.

"You have hidden depths to you, Harold. How did you ever learn to do that?" she asked, amazed at what her cousin had just told her.

"Our aunt taught me. She never told you this, but she would come and visit me–once a week, usually, and she used to bring her juggling balls. It was always so much fun. I miss her, too…" he said, his words trailing off.

But Molly did not need words to understand the feelings her cousin was trying to express. It was just like her aunt to behave in such a way, to reach out to those in need and bring joy into their lives. She reached out and took Harold by the hand, smiling at him as she did so.

"I think we understand one another, Harold," she said, and her cousin smiled.

"I think so, too, even if I could never do what you do, Molly. I could never perform on the stage," he said, but Molly and Michael both gave an exclamation to the contrary.

"But have you ever tried?" Michael asked.

"No, but the thought of it is quite… terrifying," he said, blushing, as Molly's father now seized him by the arm.

"Enough of this! You will do as I say, Harold," he exclaimed, but Harold only shook his head and laughed.

"I shall do as I please, Uncle. You have a month to set your affairs in order and leave Wisgate Grange, and you have but a day to ensure Molly's rightful inheritance is given her. Do you understand?" he said.

"Father, it cannot be—he is a fool, he is a simpleton, he is—" Tobias wailed, but Molly interrupted him.

"He is a man worth a dozen of you, Tobias, and if only you had not been so quick to condemn him, then perhaps your fortunes would have been improved. As it stands, I can have no sympathy for you," she said, and Tobias fell silent.

Her father, too, seemed lost for words, and Molly could only pity them, even after all they had done to her.

"Wisgate Grange is yours, Molly, if you want it," Harold said, but Molly shook her head, glancing at Michael, who smiled.

"I think our life may lie elsewhere than Wisgate, though Rosedene will always have a special place in our hearts," he replied.

"Then the matter is settled, but I hope you will remain long enough to see that happy place returned to its full glory. It is what our aunt would have wanted," Harold said, and Molly knew his words to be true.

As she and Michael walked arm in arm from the churchyard that day, leaving her father and Tobias behind, she pictured her aunt's smile. Had she been there, she would surely have congratulated them all, and delighted at seeing Molly's father at last receiving his just punishment for the years of suffering he had inflicted. There was a finality in this moment, even if some things were still missing.

"I feel so terribly happy," she told Michael, as the two of them returned to Rosedene as husband and wife.

"And it is a happiness we both share, Molly," he replied, opening the gate for her, and smiling as the two of them stepped into the welcoming embrace of that happy place.

Chapter 20
A Happy Reunion

They soon settled the legalities of the inheritance. Molly's father mounted an immediate challenge–both against the will and his eviction from Wisgate Grange–but neither matter could reasonably be contested. The Duke of Thurlstone had set his own lawyers to work on the matter and there was no doubting the legitimate claim which Molly had over the house and inheritance. Rosedene was hers by virtue of her marriage, and since Michael had no desire to claim it as his own, Molly was its sole custodian.

The eviction from Wisgate Grange, although remarkable in its execution, was also incontestable. The house belonged to the estate and was in Harold's gift. Molly's father and Tobias were given a month to make alternative arrangements, and it was to York which they went, taking a townhouse, and leaving Wisgate behind, along with a string of empty threats as to their intended return. Mrs. Mallory, too, was left destitute, but Molly's father kept her in his employ, even as the household over which she was keeper was severely diminished.

"What do you think your father will do now?" Michael asked on the day they watched him, Tobias, and the housekeeper leave Wisgate in a large black carriage, their faces set in bitter expressions.

"My father will find some compensation, I am sure, but he will not forget this humiliation. I only hope Harold knows what he is doing," Molly replied, watching as the carriage turned a corner and disappeared from sight.

"Good riddance to them. You should shed no tears for them, Molly, I assure you," he replied.

They had been watching on the village green and now they returned to Rosedene, eager to continue their work on the garden. It had been one month since the wedding and summer was at its zenith. Everything was blooming, and the garden had taken on its former glory, bursting forth with colour and scent.

"My aunt would be proud of what we have accomplished," Molly said, looking around her with satisfaction.

Roses trailed in every shade. The house was covered in purple and white wisteria, and great clumps of lavender bordered the lawns, the sweet scent rising as an all-enveloping perfume. It was a sanctuary, their sanctuary, and Molly could not have felt happier anywhere else, or with anyone else.

"I should think she would be. The garden is beautiful, Molly–truly beautiful," Michael replied.

"But I could not have done it without you, or Harold," she said, smiling at the thought of her cousin, who had taken it on himself to come and help each day.

Together, they had cut back all the growth which had covered the garden in the years since last it had been tended and created what they could only describe as a paradise, a perfect image, preserved like a painting. Michael was right. It was beautiful, and it would only grow more so in the months and years to come.

"And here he is now," Michael said, turning at the sound of the clicking of the gate.

Harold had taken to wearing a long green apron for his forays into the garden, along with a wide-brimmed straw hat. He carried a basket of tools in one hand and a bag, which Molly knew contained cakes, in the other. Harold always brought cakes for them.

"Cherry and almond today," he said, setting down the bag and taking up a pair of shears.

Usually he only spoke briefly, preferring to begin his work immediately, but today, he could not help smiling as though he were keeping a secret, and Molly looked at him curiously, wondering what it could be.

"Did you see my father and Tobias leave?" she asked, and Harold nodded.

"They were not happy, but... well, I have given the use of Wisgate Grange over to Mr. Crockford and the Church–it is to be used as an orphanage," he said, and Molly smiled.

She was glad to think of the house being used for good, and once again she saw something of her aunt's spirit expressed in the actions of her cousin. She had never known of the relationship between them, but it was her aunt's way of doing good in an unassuming manner. It made Molly happy to think about it, even as she wondered again what Harold was hiding.

"And what else have you got to tell me today?" she asked, causing him to blush.

"Well… I have one surprise, but… you will have to see it for yourself," he said, and he set down the shears and beckoned them to follow him.

"What about the cake?" Michael asked.

"We can eat it later," Harold replied, and he hurried off across the garden, beckoning them both to follow him.

Michael offered Molly his hand, and the two of them followed Harold through the garden gate and down the lane towards the village.

"What do you suppose this is all about?" Michael asked, and Molly shrugged her shoulders.

"I cannot possibly–oh!" she exclaimed, as a familiar but thoroughly unexpected sound greeted them.

It was the sound of an elephant, the same sound she had awoken to every morning since she had joined the dancehall troupe all those years ago. She gave a cry of excitement, even as Harold turned to her with a grin.

"I think I hear some friends of yours, Molly," he replied, and Molly stared at him in delight.

"But… are they here? They are not due to return here for years," she exclaimed, but Harold only smiled and beckoned them both to follow him.

"I asked them to come. I found they were a hundred miles to the south, but it was easy to persuade them to return–when I told them in a letter that their dear friend Molly was now married," he replied.

As they emerged from the lane onto the village green, Molly was astonished to see the caravans before her and the elephant tethered to a tree, surrounded by curious village children who had hurried out to witness the parade.

"Look, Michael–they are all here," Molly said, as, at that moment, emerging from the caravans, appeared all her friends–the family who had been her companions in the long years of her exile.

"Molly!" Algernon called out, and Molly rushed forward to embrace him, the others surrounding her and cheering.

"Molly, you are married. Oh, how wonderful," Celi said, throwing her arms around Molly and kissing her.

"Married! Married! Married!" Pollyanna exclaimed, cawing on Bill's shoulder.

"Congratulations to you both," Bill said, and he shook Michael warmly by the hand.

"We had to come. Your cousin wrote to us and implored us to return and celebrate with you," Mr. Marvolo said.

Molly felt overwhelmed by their kindness and tears welled up in her eyes–tears of happiness and gratitude for all they had shared. She shook her head in disbelief, imagining she would soon awaken from a dream. But it was no dream, a fact proved by the elephant, who suddenly let out an enormous trumpety-trump.

"I think the entire village will know we are here," Algernon exclaimed, and the others laughed.

"But are you to perform whilst you are here?" Molly asked, eager to know how long they would remain in Wisgate and what would happen when they left.

"Tonight, we will, and you, and Michael, and your cousin–who assures me his skills are of an excellent standard, will perform as our star act," Algernon said.

Molly stared at him in amazement, glancing at Michael, who could barely contain his excitement.

"Do you mean it?" he exclaimed.

"I certainly do," Algernon replied.

"But we hardly have time to prepare," Molly said, imagining the eyes of all the village on them as they stood on the stage of the church hall.

"But you have been preparing for it your whole life, Molly," Celi said, placing her hand on Molly's shoulder, and Molly smiled.

"I... I suppose I have," she replied, caught up now in the thought of performing once again.

"We can do it, Molly–the three of us," Michael said, and Molly smiled, grateful to at last be surrounded again by all those she loved. The prospect of the performance filling her with nervous anticipation and delight.

***

"I think the whole village has turned out," Harold said, glancing through the curtains at the side of the stage.

The evening had come, and Molly, Michael, and Harold had spent the afternoon practicing their act. Her cousin had a natural talent and together they had devised a performance involving multiple juggling balls, a disappearing rabbit, and a song about a flower garden.

"I am not surprised–our reputation precedes us," Celi replied.

She had Pollyanna on her shoulder, but she and Bill would remain at the side of the stage, allowing Molly and the others to take centre. Molly was nervous—more so than she had ever been before. This was the first time she and Michael had performed together in front of an audience, and despite having often practised their routines and demonstrated their skills to one another, the moment they first stepped out on stage would be an entirely new experience for them both.

"If only my father could see me now—and my mother," Michael said, as Algernon stepped out on stage to introduce the performance.

"Roll up, roll up, roll up, ladies and gentlemen to witness the spectacular, the magnificent, the world-renowned dancehall troupe of Algernon Trott. We have magic, we have mystery, we have every delectation for your pleasure and enjoyment. Watch the marvellous Marvolo breathe fire, see the animals perform, and—for one night only—an act a little closer to home!" he exclaimed.

Molly turned to Michael and took his hand in hers.

"They would both be proud of you. I know they would," she whispered.

"And we are proud of you, Molly," Celi said. Now Algernon stepped back and Molly, Michael, and Harold emerged onto the stage.

Molly looked out across the audience, marvelling at the sight of the entire village packed into the church hall. Mr. Crockford and his wife were sitting in the centre of the front row, and everyone was cheering and applauding as the three performers took a bow.

"Remember to count," Molly whispered, and she threw her first juggling ball up into the air, catching it and counting to three as Michael and Harold did the same.

Soon, nine juggling balls were whizzing back and forth through the air, passed between each of the performers, back and forth across the stage. Molly was counting the movement—one, two, three—just as she had taught Michael and Harold in their performance that afternoon. The music had begun and now she sang, the three of them dancing, moving back and forth, still passing the juggling balls between them. The audience was clapping in rhythm, and Molly's voice echoed across the church hall. She thought of her seven-year-old self, caught up in the magic and mystery of the performance. It had been that first performance which had so inspired her and changed the course of her life. From that moment on, she had been preparing for this moment now. Life had brought with it many hardships, but at last, Molly felt she had found her place, and the happiness she deserved.

"And the flowers were swaying in the breeze, the breeze, the flowers were swaying in the breeze," she sang, and the performance ended.

They caught the juggling balls and filed up together in a line, taking a bow as the audience leaped to their feet in rapturous applause. To Molly's amusement, Mr. Crockford threw a bunch of roses onto the stage, and there were cries for an encore—a request they obliged by stepping back and juggling with one another before tossing the balls out into the audience. A young girl caught one – around the same age as Molly had been when first she had seen the dancehall troupe perform. Molly smiled at her, and the girl made to hand it back, but Molly shook her head and pressed the ball into the child's hands.

"You must keep it, and practise your own act," she said, as the girl smiled at her and nodded.

Together, Molly, Michael, and Harold took another bow before making their way offstage. Celi and Bill were waiting for them, and they congratulated them on what was surely the performance of a lifetime.

"You were superb," Celi exclaimed, shaking her head in amazement.

"Superb! Superb!" Pollyanna said, and Molly laughed, stroking the bird's beak as Pollyanna cawed in appreciation.

"You really did practise, Michael," Bill said, and Michael blushed.

"I can hardly believe I have done it. I dreamed of this moment for so long and to have at last performed on stage… it is a dream come true," he exclaimed, his face flushed with success.

"My aunt always told us to follow our dreams," Harold said, and Molly looked at him and smiled.

It was just what their aunt had always said, and Molly could hear her saying those words, and see the smile on her face.

"She would be very proud of us both—of all of us," Molly said, and Harold smiled.

"I think she would, even if she might have told us how to do it better," he replied.

Mr. Marvolo now took to the stage, and the audience cheered once again as the fire eater performed his remarkable act for their pleasure. Molly and Michael stood watching in the wings, their hands joined as Molly rested her head on his shoulder.

"It was a wonderful night," she whispered.

"I can hardly believe I was at last able to perform alongside you," he replied, turning to her with a smile.

"But you did—we did—and there will be many other such opportunities to come. I am certain of it," she replied.

"Do you really think so? What does the future hold for us, Molly? What do you want?" he asked.

Molly was unsure. She had delighted in the chance to perform again, but her life had changed so much in such a brief space of time. She was uncertain what to say. They were married now, and a new life beckoned. The estate at Rowlands Park had its responsibilities, and Rosedene was only just restored. But the thought of adventure, of taking to the road with the dancehall, even if only for the briefest amount of time, was ever so appealing.

"I want to be with you. I know that much. I cannot imagine life without you. We must decide together. Do we stay here? Do we go back to Rowlands Park? Or do we take a risk?" she replied.

"We do not need to decide immediately. We have all the time in the world," he replied, as another cheer went up from the audience and the performance continued.

Chapter 21
A Crossroads

The performance was received with rapturous applause, and the encores went on late into the evening. Molly and Michael returned to Rosedene long after midnight, promising to return to the village green the next morning to wave the dancehall troupe on its way. Molly felt torn between her new life and her old life, and she knew Michael felt the same. He bore a heavy burden–a duty towards his title–but the two of them had experienced something new that night, something not easily forgotten.

"I cannot stop thinking about how I felt when we stepped out on stage," Michael said, as the two of them stepped out of the front door of Rosedene the following morning.

"I dreamed about it," Molly admitted.

It was the same dream she had often had as a child, although back then there had also been an element of escape to it, and she always awoken believing that one day her dream would come true, as it had had. In her dream, she was stepping out onto the stage, bowing and beginning her act. The performance progressed, but, at the end, the curtains closed and she was left alone. It was always the same, and it left her wondering what was next. This time, however, the dream had ended differently. Michael had been there, and he had taken her hand, pointing forward and back, as though the choice of stepping through the curtain or disappearing backstage lay only with her.

"And did you decide what was to be?" he asked.

Molly thought for a moment, unsure of what to say. Her heart was telling her one thing, her mind was telling her another. It felt like an impossible choice, and she shook her head and sighed.

"We both know what we want, but... can we have it?" she asked.

They walked arm in arm together through the garden and out onto the lane. It was a bright day, wisps of white clouds tracing their way across the bright blue sky, and the sun was warm on their skin. Molly could hear the elephant long before they came in sight of the caravans, and she smiled to think of the village children crowded around for a glimpse of it.

"To think of the open road, of a journey without an end," Michael said, his voice sounding wistful as they emerged onto the village green, where the caravans had been all but packed up for the dancehall troupe's departure.

"Molly, Michael, over here," Celi called out, beckoning them over to where she and Bill were cleaning out the animal's caravan.

"We could have done with another pair of hands this morning. It is hard work," Bill said, mopping his brow.

"Has Pollyanna been of no help?" Molly asked, smiling at Bill, who laughed.

"All she wants is a cracker," he replied, shaking his head.

At these words, Pollyanna herself flew out of the caravan and perched on Molly's shoulder.

"Cracker? Cracker?" she asked, and the others laughed.

"I do not have any crackers," Molly replied, ruffling Pollyanna's feathers.

"All ready are we?" Algernon called out, and Celi and Bill glanced at Molly and Michael with sorrowful expressions on their faces.

"Well... this is it," they said, and Celi put her arms around Molly and kissed her on the cheek.

"We will see one another again—we will come to the performances," Molly said, even as she felt the tears well up in her eyes.

"Yes, we shall return to Rowlands Park in due course, and you are bound to perform in Bath soon," Michael said.

Celi and Bill glanced at one another and nodded.

"You are right, but... it will not be the same. Even the past few weeks have been... well, we must say goodbye," Celi said, as Algernon called out for them to depart once again.

Molly and Michael watched as Celi and Bill climbed up onto the front of the caravan and Bill took up the horse's reins.

"Where will they go next, I wonder?" Michael said, putting his arm around Molly's shoulder as the caravans trundled away.

"Wherever the wind takes them, wherever the stars guide them, wherever the road winds—they go where they please. They are free," she whispered, resting her head on his shoulder.

"I should like that freedom, too," he replied, and Molly nodded.

"As would I, and–" she began, before turning to look at him, even as the most extraordinary feeling gripped her.

"Why not?" he replied, as though reading her very thoughts.

They seized one another's hands, and with a cry, they called out for the caravans to stop. Algernon jumped down and stared at them in surprise, the others halting and peering from the boards in puzzlement.

"Whatever is the matter? Have we left something behind?" Algernon asked, and Molly and Michael glanced at one another and smiled.

"Only us," Molly said, as Celi and Bill came hurrying over.

"What do you mean?" Celi asked, looking at Molly in disbelief.

"I mean... we want to come with you. There is no doubt in my mind now. This is what we are meant to do. Rosedene will still be there when we return, and Rowlands Park, too. But life is too short to waste on thoughts of what might have been, and to wonder if one has made the right choice. We want to come with you, we want to perform," she said, and the others clapped their hands together in delight.

"Oh, Molly, how wonderful. I cannot tell you how happy I feel," Celi exclaimed, and Pollyanna flew down and perched herself on Molly's shoulder.

"You stay! You stay!" she said, and Molly and Michael both laughed.

"Yes, Polllyanna, we stay, we stay," Molly replied as the rest of the troupe came to offer their congratulations.

"What a performance it will be—the two of you together, oh, how exciting," Celi continued.

"Can we really come with you? We have nothing with us, only ourselves and our dreams," Molly said, but Algernon only laughed.

"Is that not what we all had when we first joined the troupe? You only need dreams, Molly. Did your aunt not teach you that?" he asked.

Molly nodded. It was precisely what her aunt had taught her. She had taken many risks in her life, disappearing off to far-flung places, seeking adventure and excitement wherever she went. Now it was Molly's turn, but she would not be alone. She had Michael at her side—her husband, and her dearest friend. The adventure was only just beginning, and Molly felt a surge of happiness and excitement at the prospect of all that was to come.

"She taught me that—it was the lesson I have treasured all these years gone by," she replied, thinking fondly of her aunt and how proud she would be to see her now as she followed her dreams together with Michael.

"Then we must be on our way. We have quite a journey ahead of us," Algernon said. But at that moment, there came a shout from behind and Molly looked up to find Harold running towards them.

"Wait for me! Wait for me!" he called out, hurrying breathlessly up to them.

"Harold?" Molly exclaimed, and her cousin smiled at her.

"I could not let you go without saying goodbye, but… can I come, too?" he asked.

Algernon's eyes grew wide with astonishment, and Molly laughed and threw her arms around her cousin, kissing him on both cheeks.

"It would not be the performance it was last night without you, Harold," she replied.

"Then it is settled–you shall have a Baronet and a future duke amongst your party, Mr. Trott," Michael said, and the master of ceremonies looked at him in amazement.

"Remarkable, quite remarkable–but at least he is not a stowaway. Come now, we must be on our way. Climb onto the caravans and let the journey begin. I can feel a song coming on," Algernon exclaimed.

Molly climbed up onto the caravan board next to Celi and Bill. Michael and Harold walked alongside, and several of the performers now produced their instruments as the elephant walked at the head of the procession.

"What are we going to sing, Algernon?" Bill called out.

"A little number we heard in the Strand, I think. It goes like this, join in when you know the words..."

"A smart and stylish girl you see,Belle of good society;Not too strict, but rather free,Yet as right as right can be!Never forward, never bold--Not too hot and not too cold,But the very thing, I'm told,That in your arms you'd like to hold!

Ta-ra-ra Boom-de-ay!
Ta-ra-ra Boom-de-ay!
Ta-ra-ra Boom-de-ay!
Ta-ra-ra Boom-de-ay,
Ta-ra-ra Boom-de-ay,

Ta-ra-ra Boom-de-ay,
Ta-ra-ra Boom-de-ay,
Ta-ra-ra Boom-de-ay!"

Soon, the whole troupe had joined in with the song, and the chorus was echoing across the fields and farmland as the caravans left Wisgate behind. Molly joined in enthusiastically, and Michael and Harold did their best, even if the words were unfamiliar.

"We shall soon learn all the songs, Michael," Harold said, laughing as they both joined in with the chorus.

"I fear we have a great deal to learn in the weeks to come," Michael replied, glancing at Molly, who laughed.

"I was just the same, but you will get used to it, and besides, this is the life we have always dreamed of, the life I told you of in my letters. It is the life I have wanted to share with you ever since we first met, and now we can," she said, holding out her hand to him.

He took it, smiling at her as he walked alongside the trundling caravan and across the fields to wherever the journey would take them. The singing continued, the chorus taken up with enthusiasm at every rendition, and they journeyed on in the afternoon sunshine, pausing for refreshment by a bridge over a river. Michael and Molly sat together on the parapet, swinging their legs over above the gushing water below.

"Did we make the right decision?" Michael asked, putting his arm around her.

"You mean leaving everything behind?" she asked, and he nodded.

"I have never done something so sudden, although I suppose I did when I decided to come north and see you perform," he replied.

"And that worked out far better than you could have imagined, did it not?" she asked, holding up the ring he had given her as a symbol of their marriage.

"It did," he replied, and Molly smiled.

"Then perhaps following your dreams is all about taking a risk," she said.

She rested her head on his shoulder, and they sat together for a moment in silence, watching the water rushing below.

"But not knowing where we are going, what will happen, it all seems–" he began, but Molly interrupted him.

"Like the perfect moment," she replied. And each of them agreed it was.

The End

If you enjoyed this story, could I please ask you to leave a review on Amazon? Thank you so much.